The Girl and the Ghost-Grey Mare

Rachael Treasure lives on a heavenly hill in rural Tasmania with her two cherub children and an extended family of kelpies, chooks, horses, sheep and a time-share Jack Russell. When not at her desk she is trialling the latest sustainable farming methods using no-till cropping, holistic grazing management and native pasture rejuvenation.

She has worked as a jillaroo, rural journalist, wool classer, part-time vet nurse, drover and stock-camp cook. Her first novel *Jillaroo*, published in 2002, has grown to become one of Australia's iconic works of fiction.

Rachael is proud patron of Agfest, Tasmania's world-class agricultural field day run by Rural Youth volunteers. Join her on facebook or go to www.rachaeltreasure.com

PRAISE FOR RACHAEL TREASURE'S BESTSELLERS

Jillaroo

'Rebecca is a wonderful character being both feisty and fallible . . .
The author's solid and believable characters and plot . . . make Jillaroo
a widely appealing read. In short, a real treasure.'

AUSTRALIAN BOOKSELLER & PUBLISHER

The Stockmen

'I loved this honest and heartfelt tale of life on the land –
it captures the very essence of being Australian.'

TANIA KERNAGHAN

'This is a terrific book – compelling, gritty, sexy, moving and funny –
with some vibrant characters, set against heart-stoppingly beautiful
Australian countryside. It's so well depicted you'll want to flee the city
and find your very own stockman . . .'

AUSTRALIAN WOMEN'S WEEKLY

The Rouseabout

'A heartwarming look at women on the land.'

WHO WEEKLY

'A rollicking good read.'

COURIER-MAIL

The Cattleman's Daughter

'A moving Australian story of landscape, love and forgiveness.'

WEEKEND GOLD COAST BULLETIN

'Treasure writes with true grit, wit and warmth.'

AUSTRALIAN WOMEN'S WEEKLY

RACHAEL TREASURE

The Girl and the Ghost-Grey Mare

MICHAEL JOSEPH
an imprint of
PENGUIN BOOKS

MICHAEL JOSEPH

Published by the Penguin Group
Penguin Group (Australia)
250 Camberwell Road, Camberwell, Victoria 3124, Australia
(a division of Pearson Australia Group Pty Ltd)
Penguin Group (USA) Inc.
375 Hudson Street, New York, New York 10014, USA
Penguin Group (Canada)
90 Eglinton Avenue East, Suite 700, Toronto, Canada ON M4P 2Y3
(a division of Pearson Penguin Canada Inc.)
Penguin Books Ltd
80 Strand, London WC2R 0RL, England
Penguin Ireland
25 St Stephen's Green, Dublin 2, Ireland
(a division of Penguin Books Ltd)
Penguin Books India Pvt Ltd
11 Community Centre, Panchsheel Park, New Delhi – 110 017, India
Penguin Group (NZ)
67 Apollo Drive, Rosedale, North Shore 0632, New Zealand
(a division of Pearson New Zealand Ltd)
Penguin Books (South Africa) (Pty) Ltd
24 Sturdee Avenue, Rosebank, Johannesburg 2196, South Africa

Penguin Books Ltd, Registered Offices: 80 Strand, London WC2R 0RL, England

First published by Penguin Group (Australia), 2011

1 3 5 7 9 10 8 6 4 2

Text copyright © Rachael Treasure 2011

The moral right of the author has been asserted

Design by Laura Thomas © Penguin Group (Australia)
Front and back cover photographs by Peter Stoop
Author photograph by Helen Quinn
Typeset in Fairfield LH Light by Post Pre-Press Group, Brisbane, Queensland
Printed and bound in Australia by McPherson's Printing Group, Maryborough, Victoria

National Library of Australia
Cataloguing-in-Publication data:

Treasure, Rachael
The girl and the ghost-grey mare/Rachael Treasure
9781921518560 (pbk.)
Country life – Fiction
A823.4

MIX
Paper from
responsible sources
FSC
www.fsc.org   FSC® C001695

Contents

Introduction

Dearest reader,

I love stories, no matter what the form. Stories inspire us. Whether it's sipping a chardy while engrossed in an arthouse movie, or hearing a tale while drinking beer on the lanolin-coated boards of a shearing shed, stories are what keep us going. They can help us heal and they can be a compass as we try to make sense of the joys and messes of our lives. Or stories can simply make us laugh.

It's a delight and an honour to be able to share with you my most personal and varied writings, in the form of these short stories, and I hope this collection gives you all of the above and more.

The creation of stories is my breath. I cannot exist without them. Within these pages you'll find the genesis of some of the characters you may have come to know in my novels.

You'll also be taken to the weird and wonderful places of my imagination, which sometimes leads me far away from paddocks and country roads.

The stories are peppered with realities drawn from my very varied life and there's a good dose of my humour within the pages. There's darkness and there's light.

I'm so lucky I was the kind of kid who got to tack rabbit skins on rough-sawn walls and play with frogs in creeks. As an adult, I've been blessed to have been both a dairy reporter and a dunny cleaner. It is this range of experience that feeds my stories and allows me to be an observer of life. A life I am truly lucky to live.

I hope you enjoy this collection and I am grateful you have chosen to step for a time into my world of writing . . .

With thanks,

Rachael

The Girl and the Ghost-Grey Mare

'Hang on,' the young woman said over her shoulder as she urged the silver-dapple mare down the mountainside. The park ranger's arms tightened about her waist as the horse slipped over the dry shale. The girl and the ranger looked from beneath their hat brims towards the gully below, where the red hides of the cows and calves bustled through the flint-grey bush. Unsettled and alert, the cows sniffed at the smoke-scented air. Above them, through the treetops, the sun hung like a giant orange ball in the dull choking haze. A fervent gust of wind stole the ranger's hat and flung it away into the thick dogwoods. He gestured to it, but the girl rode on.

The smell of smoke became a taste. It wrapped itself around their tongues so that it was hard to swallow. The mare had blood in her nostrils from exertion and the ranger could feel the horse's strained lungs pushing hotly, in and out, against his legs. He felt his own heart bang loudly in his rib cage. Yes, he was afraid of the hurtling fire behind them, but also giddy at being pressed so close to the most beautiful girl he'd ever seen.

He'd felt that same hurried knock of his heart just an hour ago when he'd first seen her. He'd caught her with her mob of stray cattle in the national park. She'd nonchalantly waved a pair of old wire cutters in his direction as his four-wheel drive lumped its way over the ridged track towards her. She was standing by the new fence that had until a moment ago divided the park from her family's cattle run. Now the gleaming wires were flung back against the grass. Six strands of silver, like broken guitar strings. The girl's gentle smile was hidden beneath the shadow of her hat. The filtered sunlight caught the perfect lushness of her lips as she let rip a piercing whistle to her kelpie dog.

As the ranger switched off the engine, he took in her angular, slender body and the way her long dark hair was tied with a crimson ribbon wound several times around her thick ponytail. Her tanned hands loosely held the reins of her ghost-grey horse. The mare danced nervously in the smoke haze, flicking her charcoal tail against her snowdrift-white flanks. In the stuffy four-wheel drive cab the ranger jabbed the CB radio silent. Reports had said the fire was 100 kilometres to the east, then fifty, then thirty. Until he'd seen the girl, he'd been on his way out of the mountains, gunning it in search of the main gravel road, too proud to admit he was lost. But there she was in the middle of the smoke-hazed snow gums. A stunning girl in jeans and a sweat-soaked, pale-blue shirt and a big Akubra hat. A girl who was breaking the law by putting cattle into the park. He looked at the glossy mud-fat cows and their white-faced elfin calves that bunched nervously on the snowgrass that covered the cattlemen's side of the run. As he reefed the door open and got out, the girl looked down to her boots, kicked at a tuft of poa grass. Then she watched as the ranger's long, strong legs ate up the tussocked plain between them. His shoulders were set wide, like he'd swing an axe well.

She kept smiling.

'Hello,' she said.

'You okay?' the ranger replied with a quizzical tilt of his head. He found the girl's calmness unsettling given her circumstances. Here she was, not just caught with cattle on the park but with a fierce fire racing across the range towards them.

'You know that's a Parks fence,' he said, pointing at the cut wires.

She nodded.

'You know that's a cattlemen's track,' she said gesturing to the vehicle on the road. The pristine expanse of sub-alpine snow gum plains had been in the cattlemen's care for 170 years. But a few years before, with the stroke of a pen in a far-away city parliament and a line drawn on a map, everything had changed for the cattlemen and the land. A fence had been put up, and on the northern side the thick rank grasses and weeds were now whispering in the gusty wind, calling forth the fire. The ranger knew the girl must have been one of the cattlemen families fenced out of the mountain spurs and gullies she lived for. He felt sorry for her, but he had to go by the rules. He cast a sympathetic look at her.

'You know you could be up for prosecution, damaging Parks property and bringing livestock into this area.'

The girl shrugged. She nodded towards the Blue Rag Range and the towering column of smoke that rose from it.

'When the fellas in the city made that rule, and strung the fence up, they weren't looking into the face of that.'

From where they stood, the tumble of smoke belied the hunger and speed of the fire that had been burning for weeks now. Over the past few mild-weathered days it had dawdled, slowly chewing up the long kangaroo grasses and gnawing on the bleached skeletons of snow-felled trees. But now, with the temperature rising into the forties and the wind madly whipping across the crusted earth towards them, they both knew it would not be long before the fire from hell arrived, burning more fiercely than they could imagine.

'I reckon we've got half an hour, if that,' she said. 'I've been waiting for you. You'd better come with me.'

'Waiting for me?'

'I heard you,' she said, nodding towards the vehicle. 'We'd better hurry.'

The ranger looked at her pretty hazel eyes. He felt an odd

pull from her. Something he couldn't explain. He tore his gaze away just as an angry hot gust hurled itself against them.

'I can't consent to you taking cattle into a national park.'

'It's only a national park on paper. To me it's land. And a way out. Should I just leave them here to die?'

The ranger cast his eyes over the cows. They were now panting, not just from the heat, but also from the stress of the approaching fire.

'Where are you taking them?'

'Down our old tracks . . . into Mayden. There's a place there in the Little Dingo River. The fire might just jump it and we'll be right.' The girl gathered her reins and swung up onto the grey. The mare swished her tail and bowed her head, keen to move on, away from the onslaught of the furnace-like wind.

'You coming?' She held out her hand. 'Safer to go this way than the ridge line.'

The girl looked down at the ranger and saw that his eyes were as rich and dark as chocolate, and his kind, handsome face was framed by dark curls.

'Coming?' she said again, but the ranger shook his head.

'I'll get out by the road. It should be you coming with me, but I can't force you.' The girl frowned at him.

'No, you can't. And I'm not leaving my girls,' she said, raising her hand towards the cattle, mobbed up by her quick-footed dog. 'I know we'll be right – once we get through the worst of the overgrown country.' She collected her reins and her mare danced on black hooves marked like frozen river ripples. 'It's you I'm worried about,' she said. 'Main road's that way,' she said, nodding towards the fringe of trees on the plain.

As he watched her spin the mare around, the ranger called out, 'I can't force you to come in the vehicle, can I?'

A gentle look of amusement from the girl.

'No, you can't.'

'I'll let the authorities know where you've gone. But it's your choice to stay,' he said.

She cast him that spellbinding smile again and he watched as she and the dog pushed the cows into the dense grasses that had reached their seed-filled fronds higher than the cows. He strode back towards his vehicle, feeling suddenly frighteningly alone. When he turned and looked over the wavering hot-as-hell plain towards the old stock route, the girl and the grey-flecked horse were gone. But he could still hear her piercing whistle rising up from the blustering treetops.

He turned the ignition. The vehicle gave one lethargic chug and then died. He heard the tick of small twigs and bark falling on the roof, drifting down in warm thermal eddies. The bush around him eerily silent now. Calm before the storm. He tried the radio. Dead. Sweat dripped down from his brow. He got out, rolled his sleeves higher, and heaved the bonnet up. Fear began to rumble in him. A furious wind roared through the treetops, hitting him full force, taking his breath. The first fireballs of bark landed and exploded on the tinder-dry ground. Fine black slivers of ash drifted down and landed on the white bonnet of the vehicle. He thought of the girl and spun round to scan the treeline in the hope of following her.

And there she was, just metres away, galloping towards him, then sliding her horse to a halt as if she had flown to him.

'You coming now?' she said, breathing hard, holding out her hand. 'Get on.'

When he fitted his palm into hers he felt an energy like never before and a strength as she pulled him onto the back of her horse. As he gingerly put his arms around her, relief and comfort washed over him. She set the mare at a loping canter back towards the treeline and the cattle below. By now smoke was draping itself in the treetops and settling over the landscape like a sinister mountain mist. Small splashes of fire began to spread and the wind gave the flame wings.

And that's how it had come to pass. Here was a girl with a park ranger on her horse, driving cattle down the steep mountain ridge, with a fire at their backs.

'Are you sure we'll be safe going this way?'

The girl glanced over her shoulder at him.

'My granddad always said fires burn more slowly downhill. If we'd gone via the road on the ridge, we'd be fried. Plus there's water down here. And, what's better, an old fire bunker. Dug out by my uncle Jack.'

'How do you know?'

Over the roaring wind, the girl explained that she had

been just six when her father had first taken her there. She'd trailed behind him on her skewbald pony. He had shown her the cavern, carved into the belly of the hillside, like a wombat burrow. Every year or so the family would come back to make sure the bunker was still sturdy.

'Getting down there's the trick – especially now the tracks are nearly overgrown. When I was little, I used to hold my breath down the steep pinches, the way you're doing now,' she said. 'But I used to love this spur and the river below, where there's a deep pool with a flat rock island at its heart.'

'Are you sure this is the right way?' The ranger squinted at the confusion of limbs and leaves and the thickets of tall grass ahead of them.

'Sure as sure,' she said. She took one hand from the reins and held it up in front of him.

'The layout of this country is imprinted here. The mountains are the contours of my fingerprints. The rivers are the lines in my palms.' The ranger took in the strangeness of the girl's words and the way she spoke. Almost dreamily. He absorbed the delicacy of her hand despite it being hardened by work and smeared with sweat and dirt. He felt his body jolt against hers as they descended the steep zigzagging narrow track and he wondered whether he had made the right decision in coming with her. Suddenly the mare slipped and lurched sideways down the bank before righting herself. He wrapped his arms around the girl more tightly.

'And if you're wrong about the fire?' he asked.

That calm, angelic smile again.

'We'll become ash and be blown away in the wind. You could be a snow gum and I could be an orchid – part of this beauty. Not a bad way to go.'

'You reckon?' the ranger said. 'I'm not sure I find your words that comforting. I'd sooner live to tell my grandchildren this story, years from now.' He felt the girl laughing and he wondered at her absolute confidence. The smoke was so thick and the roar of the wind so loud and vicious that the ranger fell silent for a time

'Who are you?' he asked eventually, for the fire seemed further away even though a thick blanket of smoke wrapped the landscape.

She paused for what seemed a long time. 'I'm Emily-Claire.'

'An unusual name, but a pretty one,' he said. 'Aren't you going to ask my name?'

'I know who you are,' she said.

To the left a large limb cracked as loud as a shotgun and fell to the ground. The mare leapt to one side, the riders only just hanging on. The trees whorled madly about and more ash showered down. They could hear a roaring behind them. Fire or wind, they weren't sure. The mare called out in a shudder-ing whinny, her black eyes rimmed white with fear. A choking dryness in the smoke-filled air starved them of breath and their eyes stung and watered.

Ahead of them the cows were trotting and half-sliding down the track. Bumbling through bushes, hot tongues hanging out so far they looked like a butcher's shop display. The froth about their mouths trailed down to the dry ground. Behind their hocks trotted the kelpie. The dog glanced nervously back at the girl.

At last the vegetation began to thicken and change. The greenness brought on by damper soil surrounded them. The slope levelled off, and soon the horse, cows and calves were pushing their way through thick ti-tree and the world felt slightly cooler. They ducked their heads to avoid the scratching fingers of trees, and the ranger felt Emily-Claire's body hot against his. With relief they emerged on the other side into a clearing next to the river. Emily-Claire pulled up her horse and watched as the cows and calves splashed into the shallows and began to draw water in great lengthy draughts.

'We'll swim the cattle onto that rock island there and my dog will hold them. Okay?'

The ranger nodded. What could he say? He was clearly in the hands of a young woman who knew this land far better than he did.

By the time they'd pushed the cows and calves onto the river island the blacked-out sun had turned day into night. A terrible thundering roar was accompanied by explosive cracks as tree trunks succumbed to the inferno raging on the mountain ridge above them. They watched in awe and horror as spot fires began to ignite all around them. The mare threw her head and clashed her hooves on river stones. Wallabies, possums, lizards, snakes and other creatures of the bush all converged on the riverbank and some ventured into the shallows. More fearful of fire than humans, each animal's breath was quick with panic and their eyes filled with fear. Emily-Claire seemed not to notice. She was focused on calming her horse.

'Stand up, girl,' she said, laying her hand on the mare's neck. She unleashed the girth and hauled off the saddle. Then she ripped the leather belt from her waist and the surcingle from the saddle. She strapped them around the mare's fetlocks.

'What are you doing?' the ranger asked.

'Hobbling her. To stop her bolting.'

As Emily-Claire tugged on the leather straps, the ranger noticed how steady she was in her actions. His own hands shook uncontrollably. She led the loping mare into the river up to her wither, and talked soothingly to the trembling horse all the while.

'Come on,' she said, turning back to the ranger, who stood paralysed with fear on the river island as the cattle bellowed in slow mournful moans. Some splashed into the shallows, their eyes rolling in terror as flames licked at the steep riverbanks on both sides of the Little Dingo, but fenced in by fire, they soon turned back to the main mob.

They watched as a giant tree nearby ignited into a raging fireball and heat seared their faces. The ranger felt

Emily-Claire's hand reach for his. She led him into the river. Her eyes were warm, her voice calm.

'We should get as wet as we can before we go into the bunker. Okay?'

She pulled him towards her. Cool water rose up over his clothing. Then Emily-Claire's arms were around his neck. As the fire front crested the ridge top and began to race down towards them, she pulled him under and pressed a kiss to his lips in the dark wet bliss of the river. When he came up, burning bark and leaves hit the water with a fizz and smoke curled itself over rocks and ripples. He gulped at the thick poisoned air and found himself coughing uncontrollably. Bent over and spluttering, he let Emily-Claire lead him from the water.

He wanted to ask her if she was sure they should leave the river. But he couldn't speak. He could barely see. He could only hear the screeching of green leaves burning, the thundering inferno. She led him into the undergrowth, and through blurred, streaming eyes he watched her tear away old grasses, rock and tin. She ushered him into the dark quiet of the fire bunker. Then a piercing whistle and he felt her wet dog brush past him in the darkness. He lay with his face pressed against the damp soil of the bunker, while the girl pulled the sheet of tin across the opening. The ranger hoped the girl was sheltering them within the safety of the earth and not burying them alive.

In the darkness, with the muffled bellows of cattle rising to them from the river nearby, he managed to speak.

'Say your name for me again. It sounds so nice coming from you.'

He felt her arms and body wrap around him. Her voice was soft in his ear.

'Emily-Claire,' she said. 'It's a combination of my great-great-grandmother's and my great-grandmother's names. Emily built a hut down here with her husband during the gold mining days and had eleven children. And Claire, her daughter, secured the lease for the cattle runs.'

He shut his stinging eyes and felt her fingers trailing through his dark curls. At last they seemed safe. In the pitch blackness, he smelt the damp life of the cool cavernous earth that was held fast by tree roots. Gratefulness surged for the girl who held him. The girl who had saved his life.

He cupped her face with his hands.

'So pretty,' he whispered. 'Emily-Claire.' And then he kissed her deeply on her lips as the fire raged overhead.

———◆———

When he woke, head throbbing with pain, an unearthly stillness greeted him. He still couldn't open his eyes, they stung too much, but he knew the silence meant the fire had passed, and they were safe.

'Emily-Claire,' he said, conjuring her face in his mind, 'you are the most beautiful cattleman I've ever met.' She didn't reply; he only heard the sheet of tin being tugged away from the cave mouth. A strange gentle light kissed his eyelids.

'Emily-Claire. The. Most. Beautiful. Cattleman,' the ranger said again, stretching his fingers towards the light.

'I'm no cattleman, mate,' said a gruff voice, 'and you are the luckiest bugger I've ever seen.'

The ranger blinked his eyes open. Through searing pain, he made out two soot-smeared emergency workers in orange overalls and hard hats crouching down, peering into the bunker. Beyond him came the occasional crash of a falling tree and the sudden burst of bright embers rising from the blackened landscape.

'We only found you 'cause the ventilation shaft sticks up out of the ground and stands out like dog's balls now it's all burnt. Found your vehicle fried to a crisp up top and thought you were a goner. It was the old cattlemen said you might be here. But how'd you know to come here, mate?'

The ranger sat up suddenly, searching the dim bunker.

'Where is she?'

The men frowned at each other.

'Who?'

'The girl. Where's the girl?'

'Girl?'

'Emily-Claire,' he said, 'the cattleman's daughter. Has she gone to see if the cattle and her horse made it?'

The men looked at each other as if confused.

'Cattle? No cattle round here, mate – not since the government bans came in. And you'd be hard pressed to find a cattleman. They've all but gone from here too. Place was a damn-sight better off when they were here looking after it, if you ask me. You should see it out there. A fire hotter than hell.'

The other rescue worker cranked the top off a water bottle and handed it to the ranger, then got straight on the radio to tell the medicos to get down there fast as the ranger was in shock and delirious. As they settled the ranger back down, the first rescue worker talked on.

'Some say one of the cattlemen's daughters got lost up here a few years back. Said she was going after strays the year they were kicked off the land and never made it back. But the locals knew she wouldn't get lost. They reckon she was cut up so bad about the bans, she came up here and took her own life. Galloped her grey mare off a cliff into Hell's Hollow. Reckon the place is haunted now, they say. 'Course it's all rumour. Eh, mate?'

'Grey mare?' The ranger's heart pounded and his head felt like flames were exploding within.

On the chopper ride out the ranger watched as they lifted past the black-faced mountainside. Burnt matchstick trees, cremated from top to bottom, smouldered as far as the eye could see. Millions of acres seared too hot. The blackness was lit occasionally by lingering flames that still burned on the breeze-side of tree trunks and in the guts of hollow stumps.

The ranger pressed cool cotton pads onto his eyes and felt stinging tears roll over his blistered cheeks. And in his mind, he saw a beautiful girl on a ghost-grey horse, standing in a thicket of snow gums. The land was written on her palms and fingertips and, he now knew, the land had also been written in her heart.

Gentleman Required

Mary was still shaking when she arrived at the library for work. Normally she loved the comforting smell of books and the warmth of the sun-filled building. Most days she'd hang her tortoiseshell reading glasses around her neck and make herself a cup of coffee, but this morning she got straight to work just so she could block the memory of her tumultuous start to the day.

'Good morning!' Doreen called from behind the returns desk. Mary tried to smile but blinked tears away instead.

'Morning,' she said before disappearing into the labyrinth of shelves to look for the returns trolley. But it was no good trying to act as if nothing had happened. She held onto the cookery section shelves and breathed deeply. Pulling a crumpled hanky from her sleeve, Mary dabbed her eyes and blew her nose. The shrill ring of the phone at the front desk made her jump. She never wanted to answer the phone again. Not after this morning's call at home.

The hissing, breathy voice on the other end of the line had made Mary shiver. Even after she'd slammed down the receiver and pulled the floral quilt over her head, she still felt cold. She had invited her pet pig, Bessie, to hop up on the bed so she could cuddle her and stroke her silky ears, but even Bessie's comforting presence couldn't stop Mary from replaying the creepy voice over and over in her head.

'Want a bit of lovin', do you, lady?' the voice had taunted. 'Like to read books, eh? Wanna read some dirty books with me? Eh? Lady?'

What could she tell Doreen? How could she say she'd put an ad in the adult section of the classifieds of the paper in the hope of finding someone? A gentleman. A soulmate. A husband.

Mary sighed as she walked around the shelves and found the abandoned book trolley in the romance section. As she pushed its squeaking frame along the plush carpet the shelves seemed to close in around her and titles like *Lover's Bliss*, *Hot Passion Nights*, *Carmen's Sin*, *Tall Dark Stranger*, *Forever in Love* seemed to mock her.

'Trash,' Mary told herself. But really, she wanted to devour the books the way she devoured her favourite biscuits dipped in cream. She wanted to consume every hot, loving word of them and live the life of the romantic heroine to the full.

But she was single. Nearly forty and still single.

Once Mary had finished shelving the returns it was morning-tea time.

'Cream bun for you?' called Doreen, stooping to pick up her handbag.

'Not today. Thank you all the same, Doreen,' Mary said.

Doreen looked up, startled. Mary ordered a plump yellow cream bun every morning, whereas Doreen always ate fruit.

'Are you all right, Mary?'

Mary nodded. 'Fine, thanks,' she stammered.

She was sure she knew what Doreen would be thinking. *It's about time she tried to lose some weight. No wonder she's still single.*

Mary looked down at her oversized purple shirt and wanted to cry again. She'd been told she had a pretty face by men in the past. Some had remarked on her lovely wavy dark hair and large amber eyes. If she could be cut off at the head, maybe she'd be okay.

'Back in a sec,' Doreen called out.

The moment the door shut, Mary descended on the newspaper.

She lowered her rounded bottom into a chair and flicked to the classifieds. There it was. With a flush of embarrassment and guilt she saw her ad was listed under 'Adult' and ran after 'Cheeky Marie's' and 'Lesbian Action Live'. All she wanted was a companion. A gentleman. Not to feel sordid, or smutty.

She read her ad. *Gentleman required (35–45) as companion for quiet lady, likes books. View to possible romance. Phone after 5 p.m.* And there was her number. How stupid of her. Any loony could track her down. And now some loony had.

Through the window she could see Doreen labouring up the library's wheelchair ramp against a strong wind, polythene cup and apples in hand and handbag hanging from elbow crook. Mary slid the newspaper back into the rack and went back to her desk, her shoulders hunched over, a frown on her brow.

By the time she arrived home that evening it was almost dark. She was looking forward to sharing her special tortellini dinner with Bessie. She'd start her diet again tomorrow, she decided. As she unlocked the door, she could hear Bessie on the other side snuffling with excitement.

'It's all right, Bessie darling, I'm home now. Good girl. How's my sweetie?'

As the door swung open, Bessie trotted out squealing with delight and rubbed her black face against Mary's legs. Mary stooped and scratched the pig behind her ears, where she liked it best. Bessie snuffled and wuffled, then trotted to the kitchen, picked up her metal bowl in her short whiskery snout and carried it along the hallway to Mary.

But as Mary followed her, she sucked in a breath. The young sow stood as if in the eye of a storm. Scattered around her were Mary's cross-stitch cushions, shredded magazines and upturned chairs.

Mary froze with fear. Was the creepy caller in her house? Had he been here?

Should she call the police? She began to shake. Then the phone rang. Mary jumped. She picked up the receiver tentatively.

'Hello?'

There was a pause. Then came the husky voice.

'Books. You say you like books. Do you like them dirty? Dirty books for a quiet lady? Or are you really a screamer?'

Mary slammed the receiver down and began to shake.

Normally, when Mary was sad, Bessie nuzzled her, offering grunts of comfort. But now the pig trotted in and out of her flap in the back door. It thumped each time she did. Perhaps she should lock it, Mary thought. In case the man had crawled through there. Bessie came back in from the garden, hopped up on the couch and wriggled.

'Get down, Bessie! You know you're not allowed there.'

At Mary's cross voice, Bessie hopped off, trotted from the window to the door and back to the couch. Then she started trying to jump on Mary.

'Stop it, Bessie!' Mary, exasperated, grabbed the pig by the collar. Bessie had been the perfect pet until now. Mary had always longed for a dog or cat, but with all that fur and the sneezing and red nose that followed, it wasn't worth it. A segment on *Burke's Backyard* had convinced her that a pig could be an ideal companion.

Bessie had certainly kept her from being quite so lonely this past year, but she had failed to keep an intruder from entering the house.

Mary shivered again. She couldn't lock Bessie outside in the cold, foggy night in case the man was still about. She was about to haul her into the laundry when she noticed Bessie's swollen rear end. She looked from the little sow to the upturned room and back again. The penny dropped.

'Oh, Bessie, now I understand. You're in season! *You* made this mess!' Relieved, she hugged her. 'There was never a man in here at all. You've grown up! The books said you would about now.'

Mary suddenly felt so much better.

'How exciting, Bess. Piglets! Don't worry, we'll find you a man. Leave it to me.'

They snuggled down on the beanbag later in the evening to watch TV while eating cake. The phone gave a shrill ring. Mary pulled Bessie close and let it ring out.

On Saturday morning from her front room, Mary heard the rolled newspaper land with a plop on her concrete path. She tiptoed out, clutching her terry-towelling robe around her, grabbed the paper and scuttled back inside. At the kitchen table with a cup of tea beside her, she flicked to the classifieds, past the adult section and on to livestock. There was her ad. *Berkshire sow requires boar for servicing; phone after 5 p.m.* Then her phone number.

Just after ten that morning the phone rang. It rang several times before she dared to pick it up. Could it be the horrible stranger again?

'Hello?' she said nervously.

'Hello.' It was a man. It made her panic.

'Yes?'

'I was ringing about your ad.'

'Which ad might that be?' Mary's palms began to sweat.

'Oh, I hope I haven't dialled the wrong number,' said the man. 'A chap put an ad in the paper about a Berkshire sow.'

'Oh, that's Bessie! Yes!' Relief washed over her.

'Bessie?'

'No! I mean, yes, it was me.'

He laughed a shy laugh. 'Good.'

'Where are you calling from?'

'Cranbourne. My name's Nigel. Nigel Peterson.'

'You're not far from me then. Is your boar a Berkshire?'

'Through and through. He's got a pedigree going back to Lincoln Ambassador 1183.'

Mary squealed in excitement. 'How wonderful!'

'I can pop him on the truck and bring him over tonight if you like. Then if you fancy the look of him, we can . . . introduce them. If not, I'll take him home again.'

'Lovely. My address is 43 Elms Crescent, the double block with the old cottage and shed. I'll see you about six then?'

'Fine. Well, goodbye, Bessie.'

'Mary.'

'Sorry?'

'My name is Mary. The sow is Bessie.'

'Oh! I'm awfully sorry. See you at six then, Mary.'

As she put down the phone, her excitement faded when she suddenly realised what a fool she'd been. He could be another prank caller and now he had her address. She sighed over her stupidity. But he'd sounded so nice, she thought, and he knew about the Australian boar Lincoln Ambassador, who was so good he was sent to England in 1976 to breed Berkshires there.

Late in the afternoon, on the back porch, Mary dragged the brush over Bessie's black back and the pig arched up towards the brush's pleasurable prongs.

'We want you looking special for your date tonight, Bessie.'

She was just wiping the pig's eyes over with a damp cloth when the doorbell rang out down the hallway, spilling its urgent signal into the back yard.

Quickly brushing down her own long dark hair and straightening her light-blue dress, Mary went to open the front door.

'Mary?' The man standing before her held his tweed cap in his hand. He had warm blue eyes that crinkled at the corners. Even though his hair was starting to recede, he still looked handsome standing there with his shirtsleeves rolled up and cord trousers tucked into lace-up boots.

'Nigel?'

'Yes. How do you do?'

Mary offered her hand and Nigel shook it gently before stepping back and stretching out his arm with a grand *Sale of the Century* gesture.

'Mary, meet Napoleon.'

The large boar sniffed at the wire cage on the ute.

Mary's mouth dropped open.

'He's a beauty! Look at those pink points!' She admired the handsome boar, noting how his black legs gave way to very correct pink ankles and trotters. 'And those prick ears are perfect! He's even got a hint of pink on the snout. Oh, Bessie will love him! What's his nature like?'

'A perfect gentleman,' smiled Nigel proudly. 'He's quiet too. A bit like his owner.'

For an instant Nigel's eyes met Mary's and a feeling swept over her that made her blush. Both of them sensed it, standing there in the doorway under the golden light of the evening sun. Each had found their perfect match. As they laughed shyly together, the phone began to ring.

Mary glanced at Nigel.

'Nigel, could you please do me a favour and answer that? I've had a nuisance caller.'

She gestured to him to come inside. 'Would you mind? They'll think I have a man about the place then.'

Nigel grinned at her. 'Not at all, Mary. Happy to be your

knight in shining armour.' As they came inside together, Mary smiled and stooped to pat Bessie.

'I think we've found the perfect gentlemen required, Bess. Don't you?' Bessie looked up at her, and in the dim light of the hallway, Mary was certain she saw the pig wink.

The Apple, the Pony and the Snake

The day was alive with heat, and the sun stung her shoulders as she felt the warmth and softness of her pony's back and belly beneath her. She wore her favourite blue bathers, sneakers and a floppy straw hat, a stalk of golden wheat tucked in the band. The girl rode bareback along the fence line. The rye grass rustled against the pony's legs and the girl dipped her toes so that the taller seedheads tapped against her shoes. She swung her legs and felt the pony's coat of dun slide back and forth against her thighs. Bending over the pony's neck she unhitched the gate and urged him through, squeezing her thighs. The pony responded to the flex of her muscles.

The water silently swirled by, over bottle-green and brown rocks. Dragonflies hovered in the stillness of the afternoon. She slid from the pony and hitched his rope to a low, gnarled willow branch in the shade. From her bag, the girl took an apple, bit a piece and offered it up to the pony on the flat of her palm. His strong muzzle wriggled over her hand in search of more. She bit the apple again and offered the pony another piece, then turned to eat the rest of the apple herself, squinting at the glimmer of the river.

Lying in the sun on the grassy bank, eyes closed, she listened to her pony tearing the grass, chewing the fresh green juices from the stems, hearing the jangle of his bit on his tongue and the occasional swish of his tail.

Her eyes opened when the sound stopped. Her pony stood with his head up, ears forward and grass hanging from his mouth. She looked downstream to catch the sound of high laughter and saw silver splashes caught on the breeze. Two dark heads and one fair one were visible below the boughs overhanging the deeper water. They came towards her, three young boys with eager eyes, scrambling over rocks using both hands and feet. The girl sat up.

They stood looking at her, surprised by her presence. Not sure now how to act.

'Hi,' she said, shading her eyes. 'You from next door's farm?'

'He is,' said the smallest boy, pointing to the oldest. 'We're just up for a visit.'

'Me too,' she said.

She stood and waded into the river's pool of deep green then stretched her arms in front of her and dived. The cool water tingled on her hot scalp and drew her long hair into shimmering strands when she at last emerged at the heart of the river.

'Coming in?' she asked the boys.

They edged their way forward from the shallow rocks and dived into the water. Soon all of them were splashing and laughing until at last four panting bodies dragged themselves onto the warm green bank.

'That your pony?' said the dark-haired farm boy.

'Yep, my aunt brought him up for the holidays for me. Want a ride?'

'Okay,' he breathed, glancing at the other two boys.

She flicked the reins up over the pony and scrambled onto his back, hauling the boy up by his arm.

'Ridden before?'

'Nup.'

'Hold onto my waist, grip with your legs and try not to kick his guts.'

She watched the boy's thin brown arm encircle her. The boy bit his lip. The two on the ground giggled and turned away. The motion of the pony moved their bodies together so the wetness from the river turned to sweat between them.

'You want to try trotting?'

She turned and saw doubt in his wide blue eyes but then he nodded.

She chose a flat section of ground that ran alongside the

pines on the river. She squeezed her calves into her pony's belly and he began to trot.

'When he throws his leg forward, push your bum up with the inside of your thighs, like this. It's called rising to the trot.'

She felt the boy grip her harder and heard him laugh nervously. She began to giggle too, and soon the trotting pony was jolting the laughter from them. Just as she turned her head to see the flash of his white-toothed smile the pony lurched sideways. Then he reared and spun. She only just caught herself on the pony's neck and felt the boy thrown wildly to the side. But still the boy stuck. He righted himself, hauling on her waist and she felt the breath rise and fall from his chest as he pressed against her back. By now the pony was bolting and the girl was struggling to grab the reins. The rye grass shimmered past as the pony's drumming hooves disappeared in the long summertime growth. The girl's hair blew onto the boy's face and stuck there as he clung to her while she pulled the pony in a wide circle. At last, on the fence line, the pony skidded to a stop. The boy was panting, almost sobbing. Ahead of them she could hear his mates shouting and playing in the river. Their legs rose and fell with the breath of the pony that snorted and still danced on little black hooves. Their thighs were hot and slick with sweat.

'What was that all about?' he said.

She turned to find his summer-blue eyes.

'A snake,' she said. 'It was just a snake.'

True Hands

In the pre-dawn light small but strong hands grip the reins as pelting hooves pound down on wet grey sand. Horse and rider share the same piston-like breath, foggy like the morning. The stopwatch is ticking in the palm of an old-time trainer's hand and all that can hazily be seen from his side of the track is the winking red light on the rider's helmet. Beside the jockey, on the highway running past, a Mercedes glides over a sheened black road. The driver gently brakes at the curve. Brakes again. At that very moment, all of them are thinking the same thing. Nothing profound, of what the day might bring or where they are travelling in life. They share the simple human thought of what they might have for breakfast . . .

It was a busy little bakery set in a cluster of worn-out shops, wedged between the bottle-o and the Hello Beautiful! salon. Striding through the bakery door were mostly macho workers in grubby high-vis vests of yellow, orange and green. Men with muddy boots who drove trucks or fixed pipes and powerlines. There was also the ramshackle crew from the racing stables down the road, decked out in dirty polar fleeces and jeans. Each morning half-starved jockeys stood at the counter and eyed the vanilla slices and cream buns, but only ever ordered coffees. Thick-set girls who lugged wheelbarrows laden with horse manure and sawdust would order hot chocolates in waxed paper cups, and scoff down pepper-steak pies for breakfast.

Before the peak-hour traffic began to fester in the CBD, the office workers who scooted round the edge of the city paused on their commute to pull into the vast bitumen car park. Alighting from their cars, looking more polished than the rest, they would pass through the heavy glass bakery doors. There, sleepily, passively, bitterly, they stood at the counter with dull expressions of resignation, wishing for better cappuccinos, more stylish service and the weekend.

Most mornings Sonia Luglio was also at the bakery, her mind still on the last horse she had ridden. As she stood before the counter with the delicious aroma of fresh pies, bread and coffee warming her senses, Sonia would calculate strategies to improve the animal's performance for old Frank, who was well short of winners so far this race season. As she waited to order she catalogued in her head which horse nominations needed completion, what horses should run over what distance and what the prize money would be for what race. How the weather might be on race day: glugging up the track or baking it to a hard crust. On her more despondent days, when every bone in her lithe little body spoke to her of hardship, when tiredness swelled in her like the ocean, Sonia calculated how many hours it would be before she could head home to her couch for a snooze. It was days like that when her Italian papa's voice came to her:

'Ah, Sonia! You coulda been a *vet,* you know! Or even a doctor. You coulda been . . . *anything*!' He would take her hands in his giant soft paws and shake his head.

'Bella!' he would say, 'You were . . . the *golden* one!' Nostalgically he would look towards the photo portrait on the wall and Sonia would follow his gaze to her own image. There she was, sitting tiny between her giant-hipped, black-haired, stern older sisters. Sonia beaming a gappy-toothed smile. She had the same large dark eyes as her sisters, but what set her apart was her blonde curls framing her pixie face like a halo. She had been six in that photo. Ten years before her halo had slipped and almost choked her.

But today, instead of reliving her regrets, Sonia's face radiated energy and life, as if she had come fresh from the bed of a flamboyant lover. The exhilarating ride on Frank's largest, most powerful horse, Old Hands, had left her with endorphines and adrenaline zinging about her body.

'Who needs a fella when you can have something like that between your legs?' Sonia had joked as she'd lobbed down from the seventeen-hand hard-blowing giant, who danced on stone hooves and clattered his bit against his teeth on a post-exercise high. He was her favourite, a champion in the making. Her workmate, Ali-Cat, had grinned as she clipped on Old Hand's lead rope. Bawdy jokes were the way of the place, but deep down, Sonia had winced, recalling her track record with men. Both girls knew she was all talk, all bravado. She barely let men come near her nowadays. Only geldings.

Standing in the bakery, as the memory of her past slid away to that buried place, Sonia felt she could devour the entire selection of muffins, cakes and slices laid out before her in the glass cabinet. She was about to step forward to order a double-shot cap and choc-chip muffin when she noticed the man in front of her. Jet-black hair, sheened and straight, buzzed in a neat angular line against a brown neck so smooth. Ears, small and perfect. There was only one word she could find to describe that neck, and those ears: *delicious*.

She studied him some more and wondered how anyone could look so edible. His skin as golden brown and fresh as the sweet-smelling, perfectly baked bread that was stacked in racks behind the counter. Even from behind Sonia could tell he was gorgeous – inside and out. Probably gay, though, she thought.

She wished Ali-Cat was here to elbow in the ribs and nod her head with a 'nudge-nudge, wink-wink' kind of gesture. As she watched the man flick the hem of his neat stone-coloured jacket aside to retrieve his wallet from his back pocket, Sonia studied his perfect, almost delicate hands. There was a silver ring on his middle finger that radiated uber cool and his pale pink fingernails looked polished, almost manicured.

She smirked a little as she looked down to her own hands, which up until ten minutes ago had been grasping the reins of Old Hands as he put on the pace at the five-furlong mark at full stretch. The bitter cold of the early morning track work had caused her fingers to split painfully at the nails, and the cracks were ingrained with dirt. Today her hands cramped so badly she wondered if she could grasp her takeaway coffee. She massaged them together as she tried not to stare so much at the man in front of her. But then, as he turned side on, she almost gasped. He was actually beautiful. Not handsome, in that rugged manly way that men are. *Beautiful.* His skin was honeyed and his dark eyes were those of the exotic east. Eurasian, Sonia guessed. His features were small, but perfectly proportioned. A neat nose that was almost upturned in the cutest movie-star way. But the cuteness was offset by the firm, square jaw. Eyelashes so long they framed his gently slanting eyes – eyes that reminded Sonia of a mountain lion. As he politely gave his order, Sonia heard his voice for the first time. It was gentle and soft, yet still had an edge that was gravelly and deep and with a pleasing Aussie accent, not a twang.

Half-turned, he moved aside a little to let her to the counter and smiled right at her. Sonia's eyes slid away, embarrassed that she'd been caught gawping at him, and surprised, too, by his bright-eyed flirtatious glance. In the hot bakery she felt her cheeks burning pink. She must look like something a dog would drag off the road for dinner, she thought. Her long wavy hair, pulled back in a palomino ponytail, had been crushed from the stackhat and was now being smothered by her freebie beanie advertising horse tucker. The misty rain had wisped the ends of her hair but left the bulk of it lank. Her breasts were squashed flat within a protective riding vest that was splattered with mud.

She willed herself to take another glance at him. But then he was muttering 'excuse me', with his head cast down, as he angled past her. He pulled open the door, balancing the coffee in his hand, and was gone, out into the inky wet morning. Sonia watched him make his way to the dark Mercedes parked a little way off and sighed.

'Goodbye, beautiful,' she breathed.

The rain was falling more heavily now as Sonia ducked from the bakery to her dirty Hilux ute. She got in and turned the wipers on, and sat for a minute watching them swish back and forth. She should get new rubbers for them, she thought as she sipped her coffee, not yet wanting to go back to the stables. She *should* do lots of things, she reasoned with herself. But she never did. Looking through the blur she realised she was parked directly outside the Hello Beautiful! salon. She'd never taken much notice of the place, but today she read the sign on the window: *Manicures – Special $45, Acrylic Nails $150*. She wondered what a manicure would be like – or, truth be known, what a manicure and acrylic nails really were.

'Hello, Beautiful,' she said mockingly to herself, thinking of the man she'd seen at the bakery, and the way she craved men, yet shied from them. Then she grimaced as the ugliness of her final argument with her last 'boyfriend' erupted in her memory. Why did she pick such rough, coarse men, who treated her that way? The racing industry was full of them. Hard buggers who spat and swore and hurt. But deep down she knew why. Far off, in the most painful place, she knew why.

It was Jessie. Jessie with her button nose, big soulful eyes and baby-powder smell. At sixteen, Sonia had fought so hard to keep her, despite the long torturous pregnancy, made worse by the screaming matches with her mama and the face slaps from her papa. Every waking moment had been a battle, from the time she had dumped down her school bag and said, 'Mama, I'm pregnant,' right to the very end.

As if to spite them all, at six months old, little Jessie had left the family anyway. The doctors said the baby had died from meningitis, but Sonia had her own diagnosis. It was punishment for her sins, like the Father had said in Mass. It was as if her mama and papa and her sisters had willed Jessie away. Prayed to God to take her. Not long after Sonia had left too, bolting from the portico house with the clichéd lion statues flanking the concrete drive. For over a decade now she had bashed her body about on crazy half-wild thoroughbreds, and bashed herself about with half-crazy drug-fucked men.

Peering through the rain-spattered windscreen Sonia read another sign on the salon window: *Treat yourself, because you are worth it.*

'Worth it? Am I?' She felt tears prickle. With a defiant, desperate air and a mouth twisted in grief, she plugged the number of the salon into her phone.

<hr>

On the afternoon of her appointment at Hello Beautiful! Sonia parked the Hilux, and watched the mums ushering school kids in and out of cars. Some of the kids were around the age Jessie would be by now. Sighing, Sonia got out of her ute and hitched up her baggy jeans, vowing she wasn't going to spill her guts to some random beauty therapist. But she had to do something to shift this mood that had settled into a way of being. The salon's glass door was framed with bright-red gloss paint that set it apart from the tatty shops in the row. She pushed it open. Inside, Sonia was struck by the gentle scent of roses and the serene bubbling of a corner fountain, filled with white pebbles. She instantly felt like she didn't belong in the place. Before she could turn and walk out, a woman around her own age revealed herself from behind the drape of a gold and white heart-print curtain and beamed at her. She was all feminine curves, poured deliciously into jeans and a flouncy floral top. She had lively dark eyes framed by lashes as long as Audrey Hepburn's. As she ticked off Sonia's name in the appointment book with a diamante-nailed flourish, her eyes twinkled in a friendly way.

'Hi, I'm Chelsea. I love new customers! So exciting. You must be Sonia, because you're certainly not Darren, who's running late for his back, sack and crack wax with Leanne.'

Sonia laughed and felt herself relax a little.

'No, not Darren,' she said.

Chelsea ushered Sonia behind a white rice-paper screen to a small table that had a chair on either side of it, a lamp and various bottles and files set out neatly on a red towel.

'Park your bum over here, and tell Aunty Chelsea your life story. Looking at your hands, we'll be here a while. We might as well get to know each other.'

'Sorry,' Sonia said, curling her fingers into her palms, embarrassed, 'I've never done this before.'

'Don't worry, pet, I've had plenty of nail virgins. You'll enjoy it. And don't say sorry. Never be sorry. Your hands show you're a hard worker. You should be proud of them.'

'I'm not really a fancy-nail sort of person.'

Chelsea tilted her head and looked at her as she gently took up her hands. 'It's not really about the nails, my dear. It's about nurturing the feminine goddess within you.'

Sonia laughed. 'Goddess! I don't think so!' But she felt her eyes prickle with tears.

God! Why was she on the verge of blubbering to a total stranger? One kind comment and one gentle human touch had been enough to open her frozen heart the tiniest chink. She settled down into the chair and soon both women were bent over, heads together, as Chelsea focused on Sonia's fingernails and Sonia recounted the mess of her life.

'Damn!' Sonia said when the nails were almost done. 'I promised myself I wouldn't spill my guts.'

'You didn't really,' Chelsea said, as she packed up her nail equipment. 'Not all of it, anyway. You didn't tell me about your current sex life.' Chelsea shoved her tongue inside her cheek and cocked an eyebrow at Sonia.

'Huh! What's to tell?'

'There's always *something* to tell. You've got two weeks to find me a story.'

'I don't think my track-rider budget stretches to regular manicures.'

'You'll come back to Chelsea, I know you will. And the next time you're in you can tell me about your dreams of becoming a top racehorse trainer one day.'

Sonia's mouth fell open. 'How did you know?'

'I may look like a nail technician, beauty therapist and masseuse on the surface,' Chelsea said, pressing her flashy fingertips to her breast bone. 'Yes! But my forte is being a natural psychologist and people-reader. You're too passionate about your work and too clever to remain a track rider forever. Now go hit your boss for a promotion.'

———◆———

The next morning, Sonia couldn't take her eyes off her own glinting pink and white nails as she ran her hands over Old Hands's dark bay neck, then gathered up his reins and hooked her leg up for Ali-Cat to bunk her on. Chelsea's French manicure made her small hands look so pretty and she was surprised at how much she liked them.

'Chuck us up some gloves, Cat,' Sonia said as she shoved her feet into the high-hitched silver stirrups.

'Don't want to ruin your nails, dear?' Ali-Cat said in a mock-posh voice.

'I most certainly do not! I'm loving my nails!' And out of the giant belly of the Colorbond stable Sonia rode on her dancing bay steed towards the sand track, finding it ridiculous that nice nails could help make her day.

———◆———

Later, in Frank's office, Sonia relished looking at her hands as she sat at the desk. She felt like a proper racing assistant as she shut out the stink of dogs and horses, the clutter of dirty coffee cups and half-eaten biscuits, the couch laden with wet-weather gear and horse blankets waiting to be stitched. She smiled at her nails as she flicked through entry forms and grasped pens, writing out the horses' names. It was as if they belonged to another woman.

'Like my nails, Frank?' she said, splaying them out on the desk as the old man shuffled in, a smoke dangling from his lips.

He withdrew his cigarette and let out a long slow wolf whistle.

'Getting in touch with our inner porn star, are we?'

'Excuse me! No! I'm grooming myself to become the next Gai Waterhouse.'

Frank coughed as he picked up the race entries and squinted at them but did not respond.

'Frank?'

'Mmm?'

'I'm serious. I want to be Gai.'

'Save telling me your sexual preferences! Tell Ali you're gay. She knows all types. She can sort you out for a sheila. Then soon enough you'll be coming and I'm not talking Bart Cummings either.' His eyes creased as he wheezed at his own joke.

'Frank. I'm serious. What would it take for me to get my assistant trainer's licence? For you to back me?'

Frank looked at her with his hang-dog eyes and shook his head. Ash fell from his cigarette onto the gritty carpet.

'Don't do it to yourself, girlie. Just don't do it.'

'But —'

'Go find yourself a nice fella and make babies. Training horses is a mugs' game. It'll ruin you.'

'But —'

'Forget it,' he said as he set down the papers, 'I wouldn't do it to you, girl. You won't get nothin' from me.' Then he turned and walked out the door, treading on her dream and extinguishing the spark as he went.

As the afternoon wore on, the gloss of her nails no longer bedazzled her. On her way home, Sonia deliberately paid their shiny dancing movements no heed as she fished in her pockets for money at the bakery. The rain was pouring down. She ducked her head and ran towards her ute, juggling the bread and quiche she'd just bought. As she fumbled for her keys, she dropped the lot. Quiche Lorraine spilled from its paper bag, smashed and swam like vomit in a puddle amidst cigarette butts and grime. Her keys fell beside a McDonald's drink cup that swirled with chocolate thick shake and her wallet landed, splat, like a dead fish. She looked down numbly at the mess at her feet, the rain falling down the back of her neck, and realised her life was the same. A big dirty mess. As the rain's chill seeped through her jumper to her skin, she felt the chill within her rise up to meet it. There in the car park she began to shake and sob. Her loneliness so complete in realising that this was her pattern. To try to do nice things for herself, to take a step forward along a better path, only to be stopped. Not by others. But always she met herself standing in her own path. The fallen child, the pregnant teenager, the failed mother with the dead child. The ruined angel.

She leant back against her ute and allowed the cold wet steel to bite into her lower back through her jeans. She wrapped her arms about herself and lifted her face to the grey clouds, so low they seemed to asphyxiate her. She felt her tears burn hot on her cheeks and the rain sting her with cold. She pressed her fingers into her eyes and tried to breathe composure into herself. And then, as she opened her eyes, she saw him. As if through a river.

He was in the Mercedes. The delicious man she had seen in the bakery was parked right there beside her. She could see through the veil of water running over the windscreen that he was slumped over his steering wheel as if he had crashed. But he hadn't crashed. He was doing exactly what she was doing. Crying. His perfect face was covered by his perfect hands. She recognised the gleam of the silver ring. His shoulders were shaking. He was sobbing. Actually *sobbing*.

She was about to scrabble for her keys and wallet amidst the sodden smashed quiche and hurry into her ute, but the man glanced up. He fired a look at her like a gun shot. In that instant she saw the most intense human pain held within his eyes. A man in the depths of despair. Then, he closed down his expression and turned his face away. Gingerly, she opened the passenger door of his Mercedes.

'Are you all right? Can I help?'

The man winced and his eyes clamped shut again, embarrassed. Ashamed.

Not knowing what to do as the rain poured down over her, Sonia hovered, watching the rain drops bead and pool on the sleek leather interior of his car.

'Can I call someone for you?' she asked. The beautiful man, his face covered, sat shaking his head vehemently. She thought he would shout at her to go away. But instead he said, 'Get in. You're getting soaked . . . please.'

She hesitated.

The 'please' he added was so refined, so kind. The please of a gentleman.

And so she did. She moved his jacket to the back seat and got in, trickling grubby suburban rain all over his plush, clean car.

She stared ahead through the windscreen, wondering what to say. Glancing across at him, she saw he wore a royal-blue ID tag around his neck. Printed on it in white lettering was the name of the city's largest hospital. She was sure the tag said 'Emergency Theatre Surgeon'. A surgeon! How very Mills & Boon, she thought.

She almost laughed. The stifled giggle deflected the pain

for an instant. Just like at Jessie's funeral, when the tiny casket was conveyed into a furnace behind a plush gold curtain and all Sonia could think over and over was, 'You want fries with that, God? You want fries with that?' There was nothing funny about the thought. But it truly felt that way, like God had eaten her baby. Like some hungry monster. She felt the tears rise again and she half-turned to the man.

'Please. Let me help you.'

He swiped his hands across his face and locked his eyes on hers. There was madness in his look. Sonia recognised it as the temporary insanity of grief. She had seen the same expression in her own dark eyes when she looked at herself in the half-blackened mirror on sleepless nights in her bedsit.

'Hold me,' he said. Then the 'please' came again. And she did. She reached over and grabbed him and held him to her as if her life depended on it. And perhaps today it did. She drank in his smell, felt the pulse of life beneath his thin shirt. She felt his pain and she offered him up all she could in her embrace. As she did, she felt his gift to her of gratitude and his warmth flood through her. Then they were kissing. Hungry lips tasting the salt of tears, watered down by rain. Bodies twisting together to make more contact, heating up the car. Fogging windows. Hands roving over each other, searching for the essence of life within, beneath the shell of clothes and onto skin. Passion chasing away the dark wolves of death. Breath coming fast. The breath of life and love washing in and out like the ocean. He, warm and dry. She, wet and cold. They melded together perfectly. A small rainbow inside the car, their union awash with the energy of life. The rain drummed on the roof like a million fingers from the outside reminding them that out there the world was cruel. Out there lay death and grief. But here, in this cocoon, they held life for now. Intimacy denying death. Human touch dispelling despair.

She would've done it. She would've made love to him there and then in his car without asking any questions, but he had been the first to pull away.

'I'm sorry,' he said. 'I'm sorry.'

'Don't be.' Now she was the one saying please. Catching her breath. Wanting to go on and on with this beautiful stranger. But she felt his energy shut down. She felt him slide back to the nightmarish place he had come from.

'It's been a really fucked-up day,' he said as he ran his fingers through his short black hair, his voice choked.

All Sonia could do was nod, her cheeks stinging red.

'But you made me feel better,' he said, giving her a shy smile, the sadness still draining his face.

'And you, me,' she said, biting her lip and rolling her eyes at the madness of it all.

They both covered their mouths as if shamed.

'How bizzare,' he said.

'How funny,' she said. 'But not funny as in ha, ha,' she added quickly. 'Please don't think I —'

49

He held up his hand. 'No! I don't think that you nor-mally . . . you know.'

'Well,' Sonia said, 'seeing that you're better, I'd better . . . you know . . . go.'

He nodded.

'I'm Lee, by the way. Predictable name for someone with my looks, I know.'

She smiled a gentle sad smile at him.

'I'm Sonia.'

'Nice to meet you.'

'You too.'

Sonia nodded as she got out of the car.

'I could take you to dinner,' he said, 'as a thank you . . . as a sorry . . . and I'll explain.'

'No need,' Sonia said, blushing. And she found herself shutting the door of his car, fishing out her things from the puddle and waving to him awkwardly as she got into her ute and waited impatiently for the diesel glow light to click off so she could start the engine and rumble away as fast as she could.

Later, back in her bedsit, she kicked herself over and over again. She should've said yes. She should've got his number. But that dark angel with the golden hair was back, standing before her, blocking her path. What would the Mercedes man want with someone like her? the dark angel hissed.

For the next two weeks Sonia did all she could to stop thinking of Lee. She rode more horses than she needed to. Mucked out more stables. She lugged more feed bags and carted more hay bales as she tried to obliterate the smell of him, the taste of him, the feel of him. She tried to not look for him constantly on the road, in the car park, at the bakery. But he was never there. At the point where she thought she would turn herself inside out thinking of him, she at last made her way into Chelsea's salon.

'My God! You look like you've come out of a horse's rear end!' Chelsea said. 'Lucky I kept the next appointment free. I'm giving you a massage, girl! Now, come tell Aunty Chelsea all about it.'

Sonia slumped in the chair. Where should she begin? On that wet day when she had finally found the courage to ask Frank about becoming a trainer, and he had mocked and blocked her. The day where she had lived out one of the most intense moments of her life with the most beautiful man she'd ever seen, yet she'd let him wash away down the stormwater drain and out of her life.

She looked at Chelsea's kind and open face. 'Two weeks ago, the day after I had my nails done, there was this man . . .' And so she began her tale.

She was not even a third of the way into the story when Chelsea began to narrow her eyes and ask questions in a Miss Marple kind of way.

'A black Mercedes, you say?'

'And you said he worked at a hospital?'

'As a surgeon?'

'Chinese-looking?'

After Sonia answered yes to all of her questions Chelsea sat back and smiled. 'Would his name be Lee?'

Sonia's mouth dropped open, her eyes wide with surprise, and Chelsea clapped her hands and screamed.

'You know him!'

'Sure I do. He comes in here for massages. His shoulders get so tight operating for hours like he does. He's a *lovely* guy. A total sweetie. And hot body! Hot, hot, hot!' She smiled with pride. 'He says I'm better than any of the expensive inner-city masseuses, and cheaper. He bowled in here one day about three years ago and has been coming back ever since. At first I thought he was gay. But no, he's mentioned a few nursie girlfriends, but I think he's a bit of a mum's boy and the nurses weren't up to par.'

Sonia shook her head. 'But . . . that day, in the rain? The car . . . the kissing . . . with me?'

Chelsea waved her nail file about. 'Oh that! Poor guy. I know what that was all about.' She shook her head sadly. 'So awful.'

She lowered her eyes so that her long false lashes rested on her cheeks and her bright voice softened.

'He's been on stress leave these past two weeks. There was a car accident, you see. In the rain. It was during his shift and it was a mum and two little kids. He got the mum and the older one through. But he operated for hours on the little girl. She died in the finish. She was six months old.'

'Oh.' Sonia winced as the moments with him in the car flashed in her mind.

'Yes, he's a surgeon and yes, he sees tragedy every day in Emergency, but his older sister lost a baby years ago the exact same way. Same age. The rain. Slippery roads. That day undid him.'

Sonia sat in silence, sadness swimming inside her. The understanding complete. The mystery of him solved. For two weeks she had fantasised that their meeting was the start of something. A love story so powerful. But now she saw only the bleakness of the moment. The totally random act the universe had devised to tease her with the thought that a happy, less lonely life was meant for others, but not her.

Chelsea frowned at her. 'What?'

Sonia shrugged. 'Dunno.'

'You turn up like an angel during this amazingly hot guy's blackest hour, have him kiss you, no, *ravage* you, and you're like . . . *shrugging?*'

'It was a freak thing.'

'You bet it was. It's called love! It's called serendipity!'

'But —'

'But nothing. Get a grip! It was meant to happen. It's meant to go on.'

'But we're from different planets. A scummy track rider with a fancy-pants surgeon? And how the hell do I meet him again, anyway? I haven't seen him since.'

Chelsea tut-tutted and waved her buffer in Sonia's direction.

'Ye of little faith! Don't let anyone steal your dreams, least of all your own self. You are *not* a scummy track rider. You're a trainer in waiting. All we have to do now is line up another meeting with him. And change your attitude about yourself . . . which stinks, by the way!'

'But *how* do I see him? Fling myself off Old Hands at a flat-knacker gallop so they cart me off to his hospital? Then lie there in front of him on the operating table, out cold, but still hoping in my unconscious state he'll kiss me even though I won't remember it because I'm out of it and dying?'

'Or I could help you.'

'You help? Yes! No! Oh, it's ridiculous. As if he'd go for someone like me.'

'Stop it, Sonia! What do you mean, *someone like you*? Someone who is smart, funny and beautiful? With rider's buns of steel? And who is on their journey to becoming the next Gai Waterhouse?'

'I am not beautiful. And I'm not Gai and never will be.'

'You are beautiful, you just hide it under huge man clothing and beanies. And *you are Gai*. I know it!' Chelsea rolled her eyes. 'I mean you're heterosexual but also have the potential to be Gai. Oh, you know what I mean! And I'm going to drag the Goddess out of you kicking and screaming, if it's the last thing I do. Just you wait. I have exactly an hour before my next client. And let me tell you, Miss Sonia Wog-name-starting-with-L, I have formulated a cunning plan.'

———

When Sonia emerged from behind the curtain to pay her bill, she caught a glimpse of herself in the mirror. Chelsea had released Sonia's long hair from its ponytail, straightened it so it had the sheen of a race-day thoroughbred, given her a massage and facial and made up her face. As she reached for her wallet she sensed someone in the waiting room behind her. She turned and saw him there. Mercedes man! Lee! Her mouth dropped open as he glanced up and smiled warmly at her.

'Hello!' he said.

'Hello,' she said shyly back. It was as if the world around her contracted and all she could sense was him, the peaceful, beautiful presence of him.

'Ah, my next client,' Chelsea said, bustling through. 'I'll be right with you, Lee. By the way, have you met Sonia?'

There was a twinkle in Chelsea's eye as she disappeared again. Lee stood and stretched out his hand. As was her habit, Sonia swiped her hand on her backside before taking his. His palm felt soft and warm. Hers, despite the manicure, was hard and calloused. She flushed. But Lee's grip was insistent, his touch jolting, even demanding. Sonia felt him politely commanding that she stay with her palm pressed into his. With his eyes he almost begged her to not let go.

'Thank you,' he said. 'For the other day.'

'It was nothing.'

'You saved my life.' He pressed his other hand over hers. 'I don't mean to sound melodramatic, but you did.'

'No, I didn't.'

'You were an angel.'

'Well, you possibly saved my life too,' she said softly. 'So we're even.' She looked up at him with a smile in her eyes.

'Dinner?' he asked. 'Please? This time say yes. Please.'

From the back room Chelsea called, 'Room's ready for you, Lee.'

'Yes,' Sonia said, to him before he walked away. 'Yes, dinner would be lovely.'

As Chelsea settled Lee into the massage room and shut the door, she galloped back to the front desk.

'Am I not good? Oh, this little Chelsea is so good,' she sung as she did a happy dance and thrust her fingers forward as if scoring a footy goal.

'Shush!' Sonia pleaded, then whispered in a shout, 'You knew, didn't you? He told you last week and you made the appointments back to back! You knew!'

'Maybe. Maybe I did. So, same time next week?' Chelsea

said, pulling an innocent face. 'Now, I can't keep Lee waiting. If you don't mind me breaking client confidentiality, I'll give him your number if you like.'

'My number? My number! Yes, of course.'

As Sonia stepped from the salon, she looked skywards to see blue spread above her with not a cloud in sight, and she found herself smiling from the very core of her being.

———◆———

The next six months passed and Sonia's world seemed rich in colour, like jockey silks of spectacular hues, and her nights were lit with silver and gold. Before work, she and Lee met for coffee at the bakery. On the weekends, Lee spent race days hovering near the mounting yard as Sonia carried out her strapper's duties, no longer wearing oversized worker's clobber, but now dressed by Chelsea in her best impersonation of Gai Waterhouse numbers, pieced together from Portmans. Lee seemed to love the crush of boozers at the trainers' bar and thrived on the banter between Ali-Cat and the crew. On Derby Day, Old Hands triumphed, struggling down the straight but winning by a nose to the favourite. Frank almost had a coronary, until Lee shoved a whisky in his hand and gave him a correct weight clearance with a back slap.

Afterwards, Sonia and Lee made love in the horse truck with the betting slip still tucked in Sonia's lacy bra, tipsy on champagne, drunk on new love. The next day at work Frank wrote a letter of support, and the lengthy paperwork needed for Sonia's trainer's licence application seemed to fill itself out with ease. Lee backed her all the way. And life flowed. Smooth, like Lee's Mercedes that Sonia travelled in. Now she sat in it drenched in happiness and new perfume. A gift from Lee. He took her to restaurants in the city she never knew existed. She tasted food she had not eaten in years. His world was lux. His place was an architect's dreamscape, a large minimalist house on a bush block in the hills.

At first she had been ashamed of her bedsit flat and barren back yard, made all the grottier by her two little mutt-dogs and pet parrot, but Lee didn't seem to mind. When she spoke of the impossibility of their relationship, their different worlds, he would silence her with a kiss. He stopped her thoughts from bolting with a touch or a look. He told her she was bringing him back down to earth. A place he hadn't been for years, not since the death of his father, when Lee had been only eighteen. Despite her dowdy living space, they still rumpled the sheets as if Parisian lovers, and spent their days and nights leisurely running their fingertips over each other's skin. Hers olive-brown Italian, his golden Chinese-Australian. If she panicked after their love making was done that they were mismatched, he would rein her in and patiently explain again how he'd taken over the role of provider for the family far too heavily after his dad was gone. The money, the medical degree, the flash car and fancy clothes, the status meant nothing since that rainy day. He saw now that something had been missing in his life. Something real. Something earthy. Something like Sonia. And the life she lived with horses and racing people. All he said reassured her. That was until the day he asked, 'Will you come to the harbour and meet my mother next Saturday? Please.' That was when Sonia knew her princess castle could come crashing down.

For the next week, thoughts of 'the mother' rampaged through Sonia's mind. It was the mother who could undo it all and prise her and Lee apart, she thought. Surely an obscenely wealthy stockbroker's widow would not take kindly to the 'dalliance' her son was having with a stable hand. Hadn't Chelsea said she'd not approved of the nurse girlfriends? Sonia felt her palms grow cold and clammy from fear. On the day of the lunch she took her fears to Chelsea's salon. At first, no matter how much Chelsea soothed her thoughts with her fingertips and massaged her worries as she shampooed Sonia's hair, Sonia could not let go of thinking of the mother. But as Chelsea dabbed cream on Sonia's doubts and powdered make-up over the cracks of her insecurity, Sonia began to calm. Chelsea dressed her in a pretty cinnamon-coloured dress and chunky cork-heeled shoes and at the doorway kissed her and said, 'You look beautiful. Go!'

Standing at her ute with the high-vis boys eyeing her hungrily through the bakery window, Sonia was almost convinced. She could handle the mother and she *would* handle the mother.

In the ute she gingerly turned the key, so as not to ruin her still-damp nails.

Then the phone rang.

Frank's voice, cracklier than static, was on the end of the line.

'Get your skinny little butt down here, Luglio! Old Hands has colic. Looks like he's about buggered.'

And before Sonia could lament that the universe was cruel she was swinging out of the car park and back to work.

In the stables she found the giant had fallen. Old Hands's sides heaved and he tossed his head about and flailed his legs in agony. Sonia threw herself into the catastrophe. This horse was Frank's ticket to retirement. This horse was her leg-up into the world of leading horse trainers. This horse was also a beautiful, big-hearted, big-spirited horse. She loved this horse. In her shoes, in her dress, in her hair, she raged at the horse with all her pint-sized might to get him to stand. For him to live he had to stand. Jerking at the headstall, whacking him on the hip. Bullying him. Pleading with him. Praying for him. In her desperation, Sonia discovered the warrior woman within herself.

'Get up! *Get up!*' With an almighty heave and a prayer she gave it her last shot. She could not see her dream die like this. And then, at last, Old Hands gave a groan and rolled his body upwards. His head flopped back and forwards but slowly he cast one leg out in front of his chest, then the other. Then with a grunt he was up. Sonia hugged the horse. She hugged Frank. They laughed, she cried. And they walked and walked, out in the courtyard. In circles they walked and Sonia could feel the horse ease down and the relief flooding through her. It wasn't until an hour later, when Frank took the lead rope and thanked her, that she suddenly felt the pain her shoes had given her.

'You looked mighty nice,' Frank said as she half hobbled to her ute, 'before.'

<hr />

On her phone were six missed calls. Lee. He had left her the address to the mother's. Said to meet him there. There was worry in his voice. As if she had done a runner. The dark angel blocked her way again. Look at your hair, a mess, your nails ruined, your dress dirty – and there's horse shit on your shoes. Mascara all over your cheeks. You should give up now, the dark angel warned. Go home to your bedsit and get into bed and don't come back until the blackness returns. His world is too light for you.

But as Sonia revved the ute through the track's high-security gates, she willed the dark angel with the golden hair to be shut in behind them and gone from her. Forty minutes later she was driving her rust-bucket Hilux along the leafiest, poshest street she'd ever seen and the angel was back, eating at her thoughts. Every now and then a glimpse of the harbour would sparkle into view. When she pulled up in front of the double electric gates and saw the spectacular three-storey house and garden, Sonia sucked in a breath. She looked down at her dress stained with horse saliva and grime.

'Oh, shit.'

No time to drive off. Lee was jogging over, a beaming smile of welcome and relief on his face.

'Sonia! You made it!'

He frowned when she got out of the ute.

'Everything all right?'

'Old Hands. Colic. He's fine. I'm sorry.'

'Oh! Poor horse,' and Lee swept her up in a hug. 'Come this way. Mum's in the garden.'

She imagined Lee's coiffured mother sipping tea at an outdoor setting overlooking the water view, the lunch ruined thanks to her. Instead, as she rounded the house she saw a small Chinese lady bending over a vegetable garden. Sonia wondered at first if she was a gardener but when the woman straightened as much as her little old body would allow, Sonia saw that she wore a regal peacock-blue designer silk shirt and blue jeans. Her round wizened face shone a smile as she stepped out from a small crop of perfectly formed cabbages. She opened up her arms in welcome as she surveyed Sonia.

'Sonia had a sick horse, Mum. But he's fine now.'

The woman's eyes creased to slits as she nodded.

'Good, good,' she said as she held out her hands in welcome. The harbour's sparkle was reflected in the fabulous diamond rings she wore. But the most striking thing Sonia noticed about Lee's mother was that her hands were covered up to her wrists in dirt. The mother quickly wiped both filthy hands on her jeans before offering up a handshake. Sonia felt her own grubby fingers encased in the soil-stained warmth of the older woman.

'At last,' said the mother in a thick Chinese accent. 'He has brought me a woman of substance.'

'But how can you tell?' Sonia asked, smiling.

'You have old soul. Old soul in your eyes. And you have true hands. True hands good thing. Hands show truth.' She nodded and smiled at Lee.

It was then, shaking Lee's mother's dirty, wrinkled, bejewelled old hand that Sonia felt her path clear suddenly, like a cloud shifting to reveal sunshine. She felt the dark angel fly away. Instead the love of Jessie, her baby, settled on her like a gentle blanket comforting her shoulders. And in an instant she knew the choice of her future lay not outside herself. But within. Within her very own hands. No one else's. Her own true hands.

Thank you to Krissy Harris, of Hawkesbury Rivers Saddle Co and Harris Entertainment, for the story concept.

Dangerous Goods

Gloria Rogers held the pen over the firm black line and asked herself again, 'Does this parcel contain dangerous goods?'

Mavis the post mistress sighed loudly, frowned, looked at her watch and shifted her ample weight to her other hip.

'Nearly done, Gloria?' she asked, folding her arms.

The name Gloria came out of her mouth as if it was coated in foul-tasting medicine. Gloria glanced up at Mavis from the dented, pen-marked counter and licked her dry lips.

'Yes, Mavis. Almost.'

Her eyes turned back to the glaring red print saying *No Dangerous Goods Declaration* and Gloria read the fine print again.

I hereby certify that this article does not contain any dangerous or prohibited goods. The sticker on the parcel had a space saying *Sender's Signature*, followed by a long black empty line. Gloria scratched her newly dyed hair with the end of the pen. Mavis pursed her lips and sighed again.

Well, thought Gloria, I'm simply returning the items, after all. They've barely been touched. So it's not me sending dangerous goods – it was the company who made them and sent them to me in the first place.

They had arrived a week earlier in the very same package, which was now crisply folded over and stuck with new parcel glue. Now, a week after Gloria had excitedly torn open the package and scattered the contents on her bed, the soon-to-be-returned parcel looked cheap and used. It was stapled crookedly and stuck unevenly together with sticky tape.

Gloria heard Mardy Hankworst's throbbing truck pull up outside the general store, and felt relief when Mavis moved away from her. She watched Mavis's large backside rock down the aisle of the canned goods as she walked out of the store and into the dusty, shimmering street to the diesel pump.

Mavis always wore a floral frock with low sensible shoes. All the ladies their age in the town wore floral frocks with low sensible shoes. Even behind the pie and chips counter at the local football, the ladies wore them – except there they threw flower-print pinafores over the top of their ample floral busts. Cluttered flowerbeds of tiny pink cottage-garden daisies clashed with blooming blues and reds of too-ripe rose buds. The cascade of flower prints fell safely below the knees but still revealed expanding calves, sheathed in stockings, the black hairs smeared by nylon onto skin.

The thought of clothes made Gloria hitch her sagging panti-hose up underneath her flowered hips. She poised the pen again to sign her name and thought of the dangerous goods.

She'd ordered them out of a catalogue. Gloria had flicked past the floral-print dresses until her eyes fell on racy reds, silky blacks and shimmering silvers. She neatly filled out the little squares that said *Size, Colour, Quantity*, and wrote a cheque. Ten days later the parcel had arrived in a cloud of dust on Fred Dandy's bus along with Mardy Hankworst's fertiliser order and milk and bread for Mavis's store.

In the narrow mirror of her bedroom Gloria ran a hand over her thigh, clad in black stretch capri pants. The word *S-t-r-e-t-c-h* had run in red type over the thigh of the model in the catalogue. Gloria did the same with her hand and tried the word.

'Strrrreeetch,' she said as she turned her rounded bottom to the mirror and bent over. Next she tried the top. Red material clamoured its way over her large bust to her neckline, which shone with chunks of silver. She tottered in her new Fashion Marie shoes and applied a rich layer of red lipstick to her lips. The crowd hushed when she entered the bowling club for the end of year get-together. It was Bernard Morgan who bought her the first drink. Then Mardy Hankworst. Then Ivan Peterson. Mavis and the other ladies clustered in the corner of the lounge and breathed and seethed heavily, fluffing up their florals like upset hens.

Now, Mavis was taking Mardy's money for the diesel at the counter and they were both looking at Gloria as she stood in the store's post office area, pondering the dangerous goods question.

In small print it read: *eg. Explosives, Flammables, Corrosives, Aerosols, etc.* Gloria thought again. The sherry at the bowling club had exploded in her head. It was like someone had detonated Gloria Rogers' whole being. Her bust heaved and seemed to rise up of its own accord towards Ivan Peterson's already bulging eyes. The alcohol and the crush of bowling club men around her made her face flush red . . . like it was on fire. She actually felt flammable, as if she would explode into flames if Ivan were to touch her. Dancing yellow and red flames, there and then at the bar, in front of Mavis and Sandy Saunders.

Later in the car park she had felt Ivan's corrosive stubble from his unshaven face rub on her cheeks, neck and cleavage. As for aerosols, she wasn't sure about that one. She looked again at the parcel. *If in doubt ask at any post office.* She laughed when she saw it. Imagine telling Mavis how her husband's hand had slithered over the s-t-r-e-t-c-h fabric!

But the smile fell away from Gloria's face when she read: *A false declaration is a criminal offence.*

As he left the store, Mardy Hankworst tipped his hat and

smiled at her, saying, 'Gloria', as if her name was wrapped in honey. She called over her shoulder to Mavis.

'I've decided not to return the parcel. Thank you anyway, Mavis.' As she walked away down the dusty street with the parcel under her arm she was sure she heard Mavis say, 'She's a dangerous woman, that one.'

The Mysterious Handbag

Dr Posthlewaite had been dead exactly a week. While his wife thought of this, she picked up her needle, bent her head and began to stitch buttons onto silk. A tingle of delight ran up her bony spine while she imagined sewing the eyes of his corpse shut tight. Prick of cool needle, thread running, tugging, through cold skin.

He had been 'the good doctor' – a much admired surgeon. A pillar of the community. And, for the past forty years, she had been the doctor's wife.

Life with the doctor made her feel like an empty handbag. It was a strange way to feel, but Mrs Posthlewaite would often sip her chamomile tea at her sewing table in a patch of afternoon sunlight and consider her handbag theory carefully. From the exterior she looked like a neat, functional and socially acceptable handbag. She knew she was a touch on the old-fashioned side. But she was certain she had more style than the other bum-bag-wearing, gym-going grannies like Mrs Smithers, who lived in the flat next door.

The very personal and private space inside 'Mrs Posthlewaite-the-handbag' had been emptied over years of living with the puffed-up, self-important doctor. Now, at the sewing table, she felt the anger simmer inside her empty space again as the doctor's little white dog clawed runs in her stockings and whimpered to be fed.

With cool, polite distance Dr Posthlewaite had come home to her each evening. She, the neat wife in the neat home with no children . . . just an annoying little dog. Mrs Posthlewaite would hear the doctor's pompous booming laughter coming from the stairwell as he flirted relentlessly with Mrs Smithers. The smile on his red round face evaporated when he crossed the threshold into the plush flat and placed his wooden box of personally engraved surgical instruments on the bedroom chair. The little dog, so delighted to see him, danced in circles at his feet and piddled with excitement. Steaming dinners were placed before him while he sighed and frowned.

Mrs Posthlewaite's garments, meticulously stitched, hung in the dark space in the sewing-room cupboard. She no longer proudly showed her husband her sewing. He used to glance at the neat navy pleated skirt or the finely embroidered blouse with his eyebrows raised. Then his eyes lifted to her face and he mocked her with silence. His surgical stitches saved lives. His needles pierced living flesh. His skills and status attracted gushing buxom nurses, who fussed and danced in circles around him.

Sometimes, when the doctor attended conferences interstate, Mrs Posthlewaite dragged the heavy surgical books from the shelf to stare at the diagrams long into the night. The human form was put together like a complex garment. Diagrams of flesh transposed themselves into sewing patterns in Mrs Posthlewaite's mind. As she gently fell into the pages, she dozed off, mouth open, bedside light shadowing her wrinkled skin. She dreamt of her childhood, when she had helped her father skin rabbits, possums and wallabies. Young girl's fingers wrapped around the smooth wood of a well-worked hammer. Girl's hands tapping tacks into skin. Stretching moist pink hides on boards to dry. The dream would shift to her tidy kitchen where she pounded meat with the hammer. Dinner for the doctor.

Occasionally, they ate out at social occasions. Chest puffed out, the doctor took her on his arm. She was introduced as 'the doctor's wife'. Her empty space was momentarily filled with this important fact. Other women patted her husband's arms and squeezed his important hands with delight. They cast amused glances at Mrs Posthlewaite's neat grey bun, ankle-length tweed skirts and stick-like limbs. In the crook of her arm hung a very safe navy handbag, which matched her shoes. Handing her a twenty-dollar note, the doctor would send her home early in a taxi.

After one such social occasion, Mrs Posthlewaite discovered a handbag under the Volvo's passenger seat. The bag was of a curious pale-blue silk in which purple roamed when she moved it in the light. Light also danced through little opaque cornflower-blue beads, which were sewn over the silk giving it a curious texture. Irresistible to stroke. Her fingertips, seduced, couldn't help but travel over cool silk then bump up and over smooth pert beads. Although the bag was small it was stuffed full. There were dazzling red, racy lipsticks, glittering nail polishes and golden tubes of jet-black mascara. Light danced in diamantes as Mrs Posthlewaite pulled from the bag a silver comb. Entwined between the grinning teeth were wisps of blonde hair. Black silk lined the private space inside the bag. Her fingertips slid to the silky corners of the bag's dark little universe and met with smooth glass. Golden French perfume was held in a bottle shaped like the torso of a curvaceous woman. Mrs Posthlewaite clasped the torso around its waist. She reached for the gold star gift tag that swung from its neck. Looped handwriting read, *From the good doctor*.

She drove the Volvo and the silken handbag to the supermarket and there she emptied her soul some more as she filled up her shopping trolley. The day after she calmly passed the handbag back to the gaping doctor, he came home with a squirming, whimpering ball of white fluff in his clean pink surgeon's hands.

'For you, dear,' he said, handing it to her awkwardly. 'It's a Maltese terrier . . . with a pedigree, of course. Name it what you like.' Then he took his place in his leather upright chair to watch the TV news. The puppy, she supposed, was meant to keep her there. To show her that he cared. As she mopped up its puddles on the plush coffee-coloured carpet and pulled on pink rubber gloves to pick up its little brown cigar-shaped messes, she cursed it, but like her husband, she endured it. She named the dog Gigi, after the French perfume she had found in the bag. Every day, when the dog demanded food, or brushing, or playing or walking, Mrs Posthlewaite obeyed, but quietly seethed inside her empty space. Since the doctor had died the dog had taken to sleeping on the bed where Dr Posthlewaite once had lain snoring. When Mrs Posthlewaite tried to move her, Gigi would curl up her lip and growl. In the mornings, when Mrs Posthlewaite stepped from the door to take Gigi for a walk, the dreadful Mrs Smithers was there cooing and clucking over the dog. The dog snuffled, wuffled and piddled in excitement – often on Mrs Posthlewaite's neat navy shoes.

One day, instead of walking the dog to the city park, Mrs Posthlewaite marched to the nearest haberdashery store. She tied Gigi to a pole outside the shop, left her there yapping and went in. She bought elegant pearl buttons, exclusive white silk, strong white cotton and a length of lace. Returning home she placed the goods by the sewing machine and turned her attention to Gigi. She ran a tepid bath for the dog and lay the dog's brushes out on a towel.

'Good dog, Gigi! Bath time,' she called.

That night, while Gigi slept in her basket, Mrs Posthlewaite went to her husband's cupboard and pulled out a solid wooden box. Laying it on the kitchen bench she undid its brass clasp and took from it the cold steel surgical instruments that had once been held in the doctor's smooth hands. She spread the perfect, gleaming scalpels and scissors onto the bench. From the kitchen cupboard she took a large bag of salt.

'Gigi! Come here,' she called.

———◆◆———

For several weeks Mrs Posthlewaite barely left the flat. But tonight she knew it was time. In her sewing room, stooped over, her bony foot pressed down on the pedal, her sewing machine whirred into the night. She wore a faint smile as scissors glided through silk and the needle pierced the willing hole of the pearl buttons. She hoped Mrs Smithers wouldn't hear the grinding sound of the sewing machine in the dead of night, but she knew the Valium would not allow the cloud in Mrs Smithers' head to lift.

After a grey morning shower of rain the sun burst through the kitchen window.

'Time to go shopping!' announced Mrs Posthlewaite airily. 'Some new clothes, some less sensible shoes . . . even, perhaps, some French perfume.' She made sure she timed her departure with Mrs Smithers' morning journey to the mailbox, solely for the purpose of showing off her brand-new home-crafted hand-bag. She grabbed her keys and enjoyed trying the new clasp on the bag. Rather than toss the keys in she let her fingertips slide in and out so she could feel the lining of cool white silk. Instead of placing the handbag on the crook of her arm she hung the long, lace-trimmed straps from her shoulder. Her hand ran down the straps to the touch the bag's most striking feature, the exterior. It was white and fluffy and her fingertips delighted in the feel of it. Her strokes paused when her fingers met with perfect pearl beads, stitched on with precision.

As she caressed the furry handbag Mrs Posthlewaite smiled and said, 'Come on, Gigi – we may even call into the pet shop and buy a kitten. After all, I've always liked cats.'

Eliza's Cards

'Ah,' sighed Eliza. It was so good to be in the country again. She took in the hawthorn-lined roadway, lush green grass, and the pretty white chooks clucking out of the way as her zippy red car whizzed past. She hadn't realised she'd hit one until she turned into the farm's pine-flanked drive and pulled up outside Sophie and Jeremy's farmhouse.

'Oh my God!' she said, putting her hand to her mouth as she looked at the meaty mush of feathers stuck to her glossy black bumper bar. 'I can't believe it! I've killed a chook! The poor thing! Oh, how awful. I thought I'd just hit a pothole!'

Her friend Sophie surveyed the scene, cradling her three-week-old baby.

'You've turned into such a townie! It's not a chook, you dork. It's a bantam rooster. Annoying little bastard, too.' With her free hand Sophie stooped, grabbed a scaly leg and peeled the flattened rooster off the car. 'I'll chuck it in the compost. Hose is over there if you want to squirt the blood off.'

Eliza swallowed and winced as she watched Sophie disappear behind the garden shed with babe on hip and dead rooster swinging from her hand. Eliza suddenly realised she had spent too long in the city. Driving to work on clean bitumen, sitting in the air-conditioned boxes of the bank. She had gone soft. She thought of her farming childhood: the feeling of gravel pressing into the soles of her feet and the smell of sheep manure rising up from the grating of the shearing shed. There was no playing in the creek in cut-off jeans these days, no sifting of waterweed through grubby fingers or the murky smell of frog's spawn rising up from the pin rushes by the dam. She was all designer clothes and regular foils at the hairdresser's to keep her blonde hair looking just right.

Eliza sighed and looked up beyond the farmhouse to the craggy mountain, where a summer storm was dragging dark clouds across an indigo sky. Beneath her on the river flats, the sun lit up Jeremy's big square hay bales like giant bullions of gold. If only she'd wanted a country bloke. Instead, Eliza had spent the past ten years chasing suits in the city. Weekend trips from Tasmania to Sydney to disrobe young stockbrokers in swish hotel rooms. Lazy weekends spent painting her toenails on yachts belonging to various swanky business beaus. A ritzy-ditzy, flashy life. A neat, clean, tidy life. A lonely, boring, souless life, she concluded, as she watched Sophie walking towards her. The sun glistened in Sophie's messy, shiny black hair as she stooped and kissed the crown of her third child. What different paths they'd chosen. Different lives.

Sophie had Jeremy, her tall farming fella, and a homestead full of babies, blowflies and home-cooked food. Eliza compared this to her own bland minimalist flat, which she shared with her overweight, overwrought cat.

'I'll hose it later,' Eliza shrugged, looking at the car. 'It's only blood.'

'Could be a bad omen,' Sophie said. 'Bring you bad luck. Better do it now.'

'You've always been so superstitious!'

But Sophie simply smiled back. Up high, in the limbs of a dark old pine, a cockatoo screeched.

'Ah,' Eliza went on, pointing to the bird. 'Could that be another omen? A sign that I'll get a cock-or-two tonight? On my hot date?'

'I thought we were having a girls' night in?' Sophie protested. 'Jeremy's got a big contracting job down the valley. He'll be out till dawn, going round and round on the tractor, so I thought we'd have a few drinks and —'

'I know,' Eliza said guiltily. 'But there's this guy . . . he phoned earlier. He's getting off the plane at nine and we're having a midnight feast at a swanky hotel, if you get my drift. Cock-or-two for sure.'

'Maybe all you'll be getting is a flattened cock,' Sophie

said a little crossly. This was typical of Eliza. 'Like the one you just splattered. It's an omen for sure.'

'Good or bad?'

'Who knows,' said Sophie, and her words were carried away on the wind.

———◆◆———

Poking the slice of lemon that floated in her gin and tonic, Eliza looked around the cosy kitchen. A pendulum clock ticked above an unlit wood heater. Toys were stacked up in the corner. Absently Eliza positioned a pert-breasted Barbie on top of a naked Ken doll. Barbie's long flexible legs creaked at the knees as she straddled Ken.

'Pity he's only got a plastic mound instead of the real tackle,' Sophie said as she plonked herself onto the couch, hoisted up her T-shirt and put the baby to her breast. Then she reached for her gin and took a gulp, figuring the alcohol couldn't go immediately to her milk. 'What's this bloke you're seeing tonight like, anyway?'

'Well, he's certainly not like poor Ken here. Far from it,' Eliza said, inspecting the region between Ken's muscular plastic legs. She told herself it was worth driving two hours out of the city to glimpse Sophie's new baby before driving two hours back again just to see this man.

'So where are the kids?' she asked, wanting to change the

subject, feeling guilty again for putting men before the needs of her oldest friend.

'Over at Mum's. Just for tonight. Thought we could make a night of it, but if you're busy, you're busy.'

'I'm sorry I'm not staying. Really.'

Sophie shrugged. She was used to Eliza and her men-frenzies. 'Well? Who is he?'

Eliza set down her drink.

'You know. The usual story. Met him at a conference. He's based in Sydney. Describes himself as an entrepreneur so he can swindle trips to see me fairly often. He's flown down three times already.'

'Sounds nice,' said Sophie flatly as her baby belched and white breast milk landed with a plop on the wooden floor.

On their second gin, with the baby in bed, the girls headed out to the verandah to relax in the warmth of the summer evening. As they sank into wicker chairs, Sophie offered Eliza some Barbecue Shapes.

'Sorry there's no cheese platter for you. I haven't had time to go shopping. I thought we'd ring the general store and order a pizza for tea. Noggin, the guy who runs the shop, will drop it off on his way home. Sort of like an informal delivery service. Even if you're not staying I'll still order a big one. Breastfeeding mother and all that. I can treat myself to cold pizza for breakfast.'

'Stop it! You're making me feel guilty again for not staying!'

'No! Don't think like that. Not at all. I'm used to being a tractor-widow. But when Jez is home, he's a legend with the kids.'

'And he's the love of your life.'

'Hate to be one of those smug married types . . . but yeah, we're happy. How about you? Is this Sydney fella the one for you?'

Eliza shrugged and Sophie looked at her probingly.

'What?'

'Nothing,' Sophie said lightly.

'What?' insisted Eliza.

'Oh, nothing. It's just your track record. You seem to pick the least likely blokes to settle down with. I mean this bloke you're meeting tonight. Is he father material?'

'He most certainly is!' Eliza said, trying not to let the defensiveness creep into her voice. 'He's got two kids. And he loves them dearly.'

'What? Loves them dearly and is flying down to shag you?'

'They're separated. He and his wife.'

'Huh!' was all Sophie said as she motioned to refill Eliza's glass.

'No. No more, thanks. I'll have to drive back soon. Anyway, who says I want to settle down?'

'Come on,' Sophie said with a gleam in her eye. 'I can tell. You're longing for it. Only you don't know it yet.'

'Maybe I haven't met the man for me yet?'

'You never know, he could be right next door. Tell you what, how about you feed the dogs for me while I order the pizza? Wallaby's hanging in the meat shed. Then . . . I'll get my tarot cards! We'll see how far off this man of yours is.'

'Oh, no,' groaned Eliza. 'You and your bloody witchy ways!' Eliza walked beyond the green homestead garden into the gold of summer grass. A sudden hot wind lifted dust from the driveway and the seed heads whispered to Eliza as she passed. Fate, she thought, as she gingerly picked up the wallaby's sinewy carcass and walked towards the dogs. She recognised Soph's older collie, Lucy, but all the others were new to her. She'd become so out of touch with her best friend's life. She should come out here more often. It was so beautiful. The sun was now low over the mountain and the dark storm clouds were towering above her. Thunder rumbled and she felt it drumming deeply within her body.

'Awesome,' she said to the landscape. She turned and walked back to the house. She should at least indulge Sophie and her stupid fortune-telling before she headed off.

'You call them tarot cards?' Eliza sceptically flicked through the pack.

'They were free with a copy of *Cosmo* magazine. But they still work,' Sophie protested.

'Work? How can someone as practical as you be so . . . so . . . "out there" when it comes to this crap?'

'Ah, ye of little faith. Look around you. Mother Nature

speaks to us all the time.' Sophie waved her hand gracefully towards the mountains that towered over the valley. Thunder rumbled forth again just as Sophie gestured.

'See? She speaks!'

'Sounds more like Mother Nature's got gastro to me.'

Sophie shuffled the deck and laid the cards out before her friend.

'Pick four cards,' she said. Eliza pulled a face and rolled her eyes before tugging out the cards. Despite her bravado, she felt nervous as Sophie arranged them face down on the table before her.

After Sophie's reading Eliza sat back in her chair and grumbled.

'I will be in a quiet place surrounded by water and dogs? Huh! Ridiculous. That's your life, Soph, not mine. The cards have got confused. If my promotion comes through it doesn't sound like Melbourne at all. And where in there does it say untold fortunes?' She stabbed her index finger accusingly at a card.

'Richness will come in other ways. Through the landscape.'

'Great,' Eliza said flatly. 'And the children thing? How do you explain the children? Maybe it's because I'm going to end up in Melbourne with his children visiting every second weekend. We can do nice exciting kiddy things.'

'Maybe you'll meet someone else.'

A gust of hot wind picked up the cards and scattered them

over the green lawn beneath the verandah. With the wind came fat drops of rain that smelt better than melted chocolate as they landed on the warm garden. Sophie and Eliza could only watch in awe as the summer storm unleashed itself above the tin roof of the homestead. The sound was deafening. The clouds obliterated the sun and darkness shrouded them. Soon, with water splashing up on their bare legs and the wind turning cold, the girls moved inside.

'It's an omen, Eliza. It's an omen,' Sophie said as she ran to shut the windows. 'Mother Nature speaks to us.'

A little later, under the shelter of the verandah, they shouted their goodbyes over the din of the storm in an eerie, early darkness. A hug and a kiss and Eliza darted out and leapt into the car, gasping at the stinging coldness of the rain. The engine turned over and she flicked her lights on, capturing the luminous red eyes of a possum nestled in the rafters of the old garage next to the house. But she didn't see them. The rain was so thick on her windscreen, all she could see was a watery blur. She flicked on her windscreen wipers. Nothing. She turned the switch on and off again. Still nothing. She looked out to Sophie who was still standing with her arms wrapped about herself.

'Bugger,' she said as she got out of the car and ran back to her friend. 'My wipers. They won't work.'

'No probs. I'll call Jeremy on the two-way. He'll know what to do.' Sophie picked up the hand piece of the two-way radio that sat on a shelf above the phone in the kitchen.

'Jez, are you on channel?'

Soon his friendly, crackly voice came over the airwaves.

'How's it going babe? How's Eliza? Over.'

'She's sick of playing with Ken's plastic mound and she wants to get back to town for the real deal. But her wipers won't work. Over.'

'Do her pissers work? Over.'

Sophie turned to Eliza. 'Did your pissers work?'

'My what?'

'You know. The things that wash your windscreen.'

'I don't know! Mother Nature was pissing on me so hard I didn't think to check. And can't other people hear you on that thing? Do you mind not talking about my pissers in front of the whole valley?'

'She didn't check her pissers, babe. Over,' Sophie said.

'Could be the fuse. Drive the car down to the shed, get the fuse out. You'll figure which one. Then look for a black case on the workbench full of spare fuses. Grab one of those. Over.'

'Got it. Thanks. How are you going? Over.'

'Rotten. Bogged up to the eyeballs. Both the ute and the tractor. And it's still belting down. No more harvest for this little black duck for the next few days. Don't reckon I'll get home tonight. I'll have to camp here in the quarters and see you in the morning. Over.'

'No worries, babe. See you then. Over.' And Sophie hung up the hand piece. Eliza could see it really was 'no worries' to

Sophie. This sort of thing happened all the time round here. Mother Nature clearly ran the place.

'You'd better borrow a coat,' Sophie said, handing her a strange-smelling DrizaBone on the verandah and throwing her a pair of massive gumboots.

'Might pong a bit on the sleeves. I gutted the wallaby in it. Was in a hurry. You know.'

No, thought Eliza, she didn't know. She was a city-slick city chick, with a hot date tonight. As she ducked back out into the rain she wondered if she'd have time to shower and blow-dry her hair again before the not-so-Ken-doll got off his plane.

❧

Safely back in her car once more, with Sophie waving from the verandah, Eliza turned the engine over, flicked on the windscreen wipers, which gave a satisfying swish, and rattled off over the grid and up the now muddy drive. She tooted the horn merrily for good measure.

'Hot date, here I come!'

In the darkness, the massive pines that lined the driveway whirled above her and she could just make out the white blobs of cockatoos battling to stay on the branches as the wind hurled bullets of raindrops at them. She was about to pull onto the highway when she noticed the fuel gauge.

Empty.

Back at the kitchen door, she wailed at Sophie, 'I meant to get some at the store on my way here but I was so excited to get back to the country and your place that I forgot!'

Sophie looked at her watch and shook her head.

'Too late. It's after seven. The garage is shut. Seven until seven, seven days a week.'

'Are you sure it's not nine-eleven or twenty-four-seven?' begged Eliza, thinking desperately of no-plastic-mound man, who was probably in the departure lounge at this very minute. Thunder rumbled from the inky black sky and more rain lashed down. Eliza knew what Sophie and Mother Nature were thinking. Bloody city slickers. Where life is easy and everything is on tap twenty-four hours a day.

'Come on,' Sophie said, handing her the coat again. 'Jez has got some unleaded in the shed. In case of people like you.'

'Sorry,' said Eliza, frowning. She realised how selfish she was being. This was Sophie's night in. Almost childfree. A chance to catch up with her old mate. And here she was, flitting in for an hour or two before flitting off again for a night of shagging. Eliza pulled on the gumboots, angry at herself.

At the machinery shed, rain zinged in silver sparkles in the bright floodlight. The giant machines were parked like sleeping beasts, warm and dry, in their cave.

'Hold this,' said Sophie, handing Eliza a fuel funnel. Eliza imagined running her petrol-smelling fingers through Suit-man's hair in a couple of hours' time. He'd hate it. Eliza inserted the funnel into the petrol tank as Sophie lifted the jerry can up and the fuel glugged out with a heady waft and a gurgle.

'It's kind of sexual, isn't it?' Eliza said, surveying Jeremy's shelves. 'All these male and female bits that fit into one another or screw on to one another. It's a turn-on, really. Very macho.'

'Why do you think I fell for Jez? I love a man with diesel on his hands and dust on his boots. A real man. You know.'

'Yep. You picked a beauty. He's a machinery man to the core. So masculine and sexy.'

And suddenly Eliza wished for a machinery man herself. She longed to know what it was like to kiss a man who didn't smell of the latest scent *pour l'homme*. To feel a rugged jawline, rough with stubble, and have work-worn hands on her skin. To find a man whose eyes creased with the sun and who had not a scrap of vanity in his soul.

'I'd better go. His plane will be halfway here,' she said, almost reluctantly this time. 'Want a lift back up to the house?'

Sophie shook her head.

'Nah, I'll walk. I love it when it pours like this.'

The girls hugged, and again Eliza drove off into the wet, dark night. Her foot hit the brakes hard. At the top of the drive, the little car fishtailed and stopped just short of the giant tree trunk that lay across her path. Eliza sat breathing heavily, listening to the swish and drag of the wipers. Through the falling rain she watched the headlights capture spindly pine needles swirling madly in the wind. She clutched the steering wheel. That was close. Very close. She sucked in a breath. Shaken, she sat for a time before looking to see if she could drive around the fallen pine tree. But it was completely blocking the drive.

'That's the third time,' Sophie said, offering Eliza another gin. 'Mother Nature is telling you not to leave here tonight. It's an omen. It's not safe. Three times. It's a message.'

'But my date! My hot juicy date?'

'If you insist I can get the tractor and the chain and drag it out of the way for you. Do you want me to do that? But if you die in a car accident between here and town, don't blame me. You've had enough messages for you to stay.'

'I won't be able to blame you if I'm dead, will I?'

'Don't make jokes. You know what I mean. This is a serious message. You are not meant to leave tonight, Eliza.'

Eliza thought of Sophie's baby, sleeping in the nursery, who would be awake in just an hour for another feed. Sophie had enough on her plate. She didn't need to be out on a night like this hauling a giant tree off her drive, just so she, Eliza, could go and shag some high-flier. She nodded. Sophie was right. She should stay.

'Can I use your phone then? Ring him. He's only down here for one night.' Of course, his phone was switched off so she left a message.

'Oh, stuff him,' she said, slamming the receiver down.

'That's it then,' said Sophie. 'It's officially a girls' night in. Let's get cracking!' She began to rummage in the kitchen cupboard and pulled out a breast pump. 'Ta-da!' she said, holding it up proudly.

'What the . . . ?'

'Express milk now, get drunk now, feed baby Mummy's wholesome alcohol-free milk in bottle later. Perfect.' She sat down on the couch and plugged in the pump. Bottle in place, breast in place, the pump set off with a groan and then loudly and rhythmically began to suck milk from Sophie's breast.

'My hot night out with a hot-rod has somehow turned into some sick lesbian fantasy,' said Eliza wryly, looking at Sophie's plump white breast.

'Get over it. Mother Nature has saved your life.'

'Well, where's my cock-or-two, like she promised?'

Then the phone rang.

'I'll get it,' offered Eliza.

It was Noggin from the shop.

'River's burst its banks so I can't deliver your pizza. Flood's made it over the road in the dip just out of town. Tell Soph I'm sorry 'bout her pizza, but we can't help the weather.'

'No, we certainly can't,' agreed Eliza before she hung up.

'No pizza?' asked Sophie, switching to the other breast.

'Nup.'

'Baked beans on toast then?' Sophie asked. A vision of

the midnight room service feast of oysters and caviar that she would now never eat flashed before Eliza's eyes. Strangely, she felt almost relieved. Sitting with her friend on the couch eating baked beans on toast seemed like the right place to be.

'Shall we light the fire too?' Eliza asked eagerly. 'Make a proper rainy night of it?'

'Yes! And I've taped all the *McLeod's Daughters* episodes. We could watch them . . . perve on Alex Ryan. Oh, to die for!'

'Mmm,' said Eliza, suddenly excited. 'And Dave the vet. Just so yum.'

'I thought you were into suits?'

'Mother Nature just might have converted me. I like a man who'll take her on . . . When I think of getting a glimpse of your husband's giant machinery, so . . . robust, I get the shivers.'

'Oh, you do, you do. I just love a massive tractor.'

'Mmm. Me too. I think, now, me too.'

The gin bottle was empty. They were wheezing and snorting like pigs as they freeze-framed the vet's backside on the TV screen for the tenth time when a knock at the door sent them screeching into each other's arms.

'Who the hell is that?' said Eliza. 'The tree! The flood? How did they get in here? Are you sure it's not a serial killer?'

'I'll get it,' said Sophie, who was clearly not frightened by the strange after-hours visit. She flicked on the light and opened the door.

'Pizza delivery!' exclaimed a tall man, sitting the box down on the kitchen table. Sophie clapped her hands.

'You legend! But how . . . ?'

'Saw Noggin from the shop,' he said. 'I was bringing my tractor back home, so I offered to drop your tucker in. Got the dual wheels on her so she's high enough to clear the flood. Shifted that tree for you too. Big bugger. She's got the horse-power to move something that large. Should see the size of the chain I had to use. Lucky I had it handy. Pizza might be a bit cold though.'

The man took off his rain-darkened Akubra hat and shook off his oilskin coat. Eliza drank him in. The size of him. The flash of his blue eyes, the bloom of dark stubble over his square handsome jaw. She swallowed. Lightning flashed right outside the door and suddenly all the lights went out and the TV fizzed to black. Thunder roared in Eliza's ears as she sat in the darkness. The image of the handsome man was etched in her mind. Then she heard Sophie say, 'Hang on. I'll get the candles.' As the flames flickered to life, Sophie waved the match in Eliza's direction.

'This is my friend Eliza. She's staying the night.'

The man looked straight into Eliza's eyes. Lightning and thunder again. This time in Eliza's heart.

'Weekend,' Eliza said, a smile coming to her lips. 'I'm staying the weekend.'

'Looks like I am too,' he said with a glint in his eye. 'I just heard on the two-way that the river's cut me off from my house. Can't get back there. I've got a couple of kelpies in the tractor that need a kennel too. That's if you don't mind?' he said, turning to Sophie.

'Not at all,' she said, smiling knowingly. Then she turned to Eliza. 'This, by the way, is our neighbour, Owen. Owen the omen. A good omen, that is.'

'Pleased to meet you, Owen,' said Eliza smiling, 'I'll help you settle your dogs in the pens while you show me your massive tractor. I love a good tractor.'

Feathers and Fast Horses

Emily's mother Gillian was off and racing in a swathe of royal purple silk, bustling to the ute carrying baskets and eskys in readiness for Melbourne Cup Day. So bright was Gillian's dress Emily could see her from where she sat on her horse in the mountain paddock. Even Emily's grey mare pricked her ears and stared in wonder at the distant shimmering purple sight.

'Come on,' Emily said, gathering up Snowgum's reins. 'She'll be spewing we're so late.' She urged the sweating mare into a loping canter along the ridge line, heading for home. The adrenaline was still coursing through her and her breath was coming fast. It had been a close shave today. She'd nearly been caught.

Outside the homestead Gillian marched towards her and handed her a green supermarket bag.

'Where have you been?'

'Checking cows and calves,' Emily said, trying not to flush red from guilt.

'You'd better not have been in the national park again. It'll be a police matter before you know it.'

'Park!' Emily snorted in disgust. 'It was a mountain and now it's a mess.'

Ignoring her, Gillian called over her shoulder on her way to the ute, 'I found you a dress. It's hanging on the bathroom door. So there's no excuse. And don't forget to wash your hair.'

Emily rolled her eyes. The last thing she wanted to do was go to a Melbourne Cup Day luncheon with the old chooks at the community club. Worse still, the women would be spending the morning drinking champagne and making fascinators to wear on their heads. It was going to be excruciating.

Couldn't her mother see she just wanted to be left alone on the farm? Ever since the government had banned cattle grazing on their family's mountain runs, Emily had grieved the loss. She no longer spent whole weeks at a time with her father amidst the snow gums on droving trips. She missed her dad sorely now he worked off-farm, and the more her mother tried to cover up the hurt, the angrier Emily felt.

'Please don't roll your eyes like that,' said Gillian as she rummaged around in the ute, her large purple bottom gleaming in the bright sunlight. 'I need you to drive the bus. You're the only one with a truck licence.'

'But that's the point. It's a truck licence, Mum. I'm not licensed to drive a bus.'

'If you can drive a truck, you can drive a bus. Come on! Put that in the front please,' she said gesturing to the Woolies bag. 'I don't want it to blow about on the back.'

Emily peered inside.

'Oh my God! What's that?' she said when she saw the mass of light-as-air feathers within.

'That is the remains of Roger. Found him dead on the roost this morning. It would have to be my *younger* Silky rooster. The hens must've pecked him to death.'

'Poor bloke,' Emily said, pulling a face at the snow-white feathers, 'to end up as decoration on race day.' She shook her head. In the interests of fashion, her mother had plucked a dead Silky bantam rooster for a fascinator. 'You can't take him to the craft workshop!'

'But it would be a crime not to use such lovely feathers,' Gillian said, snatching the bag back again. 'Shower,' she said. 'Now.'

───◆───

Fumes billowed from the exhaust as Bob yelled to Emily, 'Give her more throttle!' With an oil-stained rag in his back pocket and shifter in hand, he frowned as Emily awkwardly pressed the accelerator down in her high strappy shoes. The old bus engine hiccupped, coughed and then rumbled to pitiful-sounding life. Bob gave her the thumbs up. 'Sorry I can't take 'em meself.' He handed her some ear plugs. 'You might need these.'

'Thanks,' said Emily.

Bob shrugged apologetically. 'What fella would want to drive a busload of cackling women when you could quietly sink a race-day beer at the golf club, eh?'

Emily nodded, grating the bus into first gear, the way Bob had shown her.

—◆—

Five minutes later Emily parked outside the squat weather-board hall, and summoned her strength before going inside. The women were on their second bottle of champagne and their voices were echoing in the rafters like feeding time in a chicken shed. Brightly dyed feathers and sequins were scattered over the table tops and the glue gun had cast a chemical smell about the room. The women looked up from their fascinator-making, fell silent for a second, then let out a collective 'Oooh!' as they admired Emily's dress. It was one of Gillian's old ones, dragged out from a chest in the attic, still smelling of mothballs.

'What a transformation! Very Audrey Hepburn,' said Vera Thompson as she stroked the vintage cream silk and the long satin gloves Emily carried. The dress had a neat empire bustline and a high-rise hemline to make the men ogle.

'Gosh, Gillian, you were tiny back then.' Vera gave Gillian a 'What happened?' glance. 'Pity there aren't any dark horses to race you home, Emily, like your father did with your mother after the Young Farmers' party!' she said as she held a black fascinator up to Emily's dark hair.

'No, not that one,' said Betty Jones. 'All wrong. The colour's too strong for the dress. Looks like a crow died on her head. How about the Silky rooster Gillian brought with her? What do you think, Gill?'

Gillian clapped her hands. 'Yes! Perfect! Perhaps add a pastel-blue feather or a soft beige.'

Through gritted teeth Emily said, 'I am not wearing Mum's Silky cock on my head!'

The women tittered, quickly gathering up hair combs and feathers, fussing around Emily.

As they drained the champagne dregs, the ladies decided to get more 'supplies' from the pub, sending Mavis on a mission.

'Empty beer cans would definitely look good in our designs,' suggested Vera. 'That'd be a cack.'

'I could do with a laugh,' said Emily.

Vera looked at Emily sympathetically and with a cigarette-dry voice said, 'Still not over the grazing bans?'

Emily shook her head.

'Love mends broken hearts, you know. You'll back a winner soon, I'm sure.'

'Well, word's out there's a new fella round town,' Barbara Peters chipped in. 'He's living in one of the government residentials. A park ranger. Looks great in uniform. As handsome as he is tall.'

'She's a mountain cattleman's daughter!' said Vera. 'That'd be like dating the enemy.'

'That's the trouble,' said Gillian. 'I keep telling her the parkies aren't the enemy, but still she goes up there baiting them. It's something she's just got to get used to. The law is the law. Just like her father – too proud for her own good.'

'What would you know, Mum?' said Emily. 'You haven't seen the government's version of land management – it's a mess!'

Vera put her large, creased hand on Emily's arm and said gently, 'Barb was just saying the new ranger seems nice. That's all. We don't have to go over that old ground today. It's Cup Day – have some fun.'

'Park ranger or not, he could be a real winner,' said Barb, wiggling her bushy eyebrows suggestively.

'It's not important if he's a winner or not,' said Vera. 'Emily wants a stayer. Don't you, dear?'

The women all laughed and Emily flushed as she thought of the poor ranger, who had been anything but a stayer that morning when his four-wheel drive had come up against her horse on that kind of mountain terrain.

At that moment, Mavis returned from the pub and the

women rushed to help her with her load of 'ladies beverages'.

After pouring the frothing drinks into delicate hall tea-cups and toasting Cup Day, the women's creativity was really unleashed. Like a runaway herd of cows, they became loud and unruly, crashing through the barriers of decorum, their fashion sense fleeing. They began gluing in a frenzy. Empty black and yellow rum cans became feature items for fascinators. Adorned with plumes and flowers, the cans became crowns.

An hour later Gillian shouted, 'We'd better shake a tail feather if we're to make it to the club for lunch!'

As they rushed for the bus, high on glue fumes and each other's company, Gillian looked as if she wore a red-sailed junk on her head and the others resembled Moulin Rouge extras after a bottle-shop raid.

They'd only travelled twenty minutes along the dusty road when Emily heard the inevitable call from the ladies. 'Wee stop! We need a wee stop!' She looked in her rear-vision mirror to glimpse a sea of hopeful faces, their coiffed hairdos topped by outrageous feathered, sequinned and flowered headdresses. Emily pulled to a halt and the women tumbled out, tiptoe-ing in their high heels into a nature reserve of bristly shrubs and flowering yellow wattles, guarded by shiny government signage. She watched as bright-orange, luminous green, fire-engine red and hot-pink plumage bobbed up and down not so discreetly behind the bushes, the movements underscored by shrieks and giggles.

'Hurry up!' she yelled. 'We'll miss the Cup.'

But the women were chattering and screeching in the bushes like birds of paradise in a jungle. It was then that Emily saw with dread the park ranger's white four-wheel drive coming around the corner and pulling up behind the bus.

In the mirror she watched as long, tanned, muscular legs ending in laced workboots landed solidly on the ground. Then the rest of the ranger uncurled himself from the cab. She saw that he was lithe and very tall, with dark curls beneath his sweat-stained hat.

As he walked towards her, Emily took in his sculpted features. His coffee-coloured eyes were framed with long black lashes and his skin had the rich warm sheen of polished wood. She felt a sudden jolt of attraction when he poked his head in the bus and stared at her. But his eyes didn't remain on her face. Instead they travelled up above her head, following the towering plume of white that hovered above her like a cumulus cloud.

'Excuse me, but is that a chicken on your head?' he asked, distracted from his original intention of enquiring if they were damsels in distress. The women shrieked as they realised a male was in their presence, and Emily watched feathers wobble behind the bushes.

'Ah, no. It's the arse-end of my mum's Silky bantam rooster,' she said. 'So, technically, I have a cock on my head.'

'Right.' He turned to glimpse the feathered heads. 'You do

realise that's a nature reserve? Members of the public aren't supposed to be in there.'

'Well, but what can you do? When a girl's gotta go she's gotta go,' Emily said, trying to seem haughty, even with a rooster on her head.

'I'm sorry, but you'll have to tell them they can't wee in the reserve. It could upset the pH balance of the soil.'

Emily's mouth dropped open. She was about to deliver her spiel on 'government types and bureaucratic regulations' when she noticed the twinkle in the ranger's eye.

'Lucky it's not duck season. They could be in real trouble,' he said, his face lighting up in a big, heart-melting grin. 'What with the equine flu and bird flu getting about, it's a wonder you're allowed to transport them!'

They both burst out laughing.

'I'm Andrew, by the way.'

'Emily.'

'You look familiar.' The ranger's eyes narrowed. 'But maybe it's just that I've met your rooster before.'

Emily swallowed, recalling her ride that morning in the national park.

'I'm sure we've never met,' she said quickly as she started the sluggish engine.

He tapped the side of the bus. 'Well, enjoy the rest of the day.'

Just then, Vera staggered from the bushes, crowing, 'Oooh!

Emily's found a fella! Hey, Em, remember a silky cock on the head is worth two in the bush.' And the other women screeched with laughter.

As she drove on, Emily shut out the noisy women, thinking only of the gorgeous ranger. Guiltily she relived her morning ride with Snowgum. She'd aimed the mare at the park's boom gate, clearing the orange metal bar easily. At a jog they had made their way along the track, Emily taking note of the overgrown tracks and tall rank grasses.

For generations her family had cared for this land. Now they'd been locked out – and look what the land had become in their absence. Her grandfather had taught her how fires that burnt too hot destroyed rather than rejuvenated, and how holistic grazing management and natural manuring helped the delicate soils and the rarer species find sunlight to compete with the more robust grasses.

At the top of the craggy bluff, she'd drawn up her horse to breathe in a spectacular view across their remaining cattle run on the foothills. The strong wind meant she hadn't heard the vehicle approaching until it was only a few metres away. She and Snowgum had spun round, startled. Seeing the four-wheel drive with the formal logo on the door, Emily had panicked. Just like in the movies, she'd kicked Snowgum into a race-day leap, galloping off down the track. Glancing over her shoulder, she'd seen the ranger in hot pursuit. She heard his engine revving as he lumped his way over the rough track.

Snowgum crashed through overgrown tussocks, scrambled over rocks, and, just when the ranger was gaining on them, leapt from a boulder down the mountainside. Skidding down over a scree slope, Emily found herself in the thick of twisted gums. Snowgum had weaved expertly through trees and scrub, finding the lower track, and then sailed over the boom gate that drew the line between park and private land. It was here Emily had pulled up her horse to turn and wave cheekily to the ranger, who was creeping his way down the steep rutted track above them. Then she had cantered away, her breath catching and her heart drumming.

───────◆───────

Now Emily was feeling a different wave of nerves. Something was clunking loudly and the bus could barely drag itself along over sixty k's. She changed down gears at the corners, every turn prompting a sway of feathers as the ladies gripped the seats. Then, like a thunder clap, there was a deafening bang. The bus sat down like a dog on the road. Backsides jarred against seats. Women screamed. Hands clutched for balance. Feathers flew. Dust billowed. And Emily watched as the two back wheels went spearing off into the roadside wattles. Startled, the women sat for a time, making sure everyone was all right. Then they filed out of the bus, fascinators askew, but handbags intact.

In her Audrey Hepburn-style dress on the red gravel road, Emily stooped to look under the bus. 'Back axle's snapped.'

The women stood about, debating what to do, but soon they heard a vehicle approaching. The ranger again. This time with a trailer and crate in tow.

'Ah,' he said cheerily. 'Now my damsels really are in distress!'

He helped each one onto the trailer, taking their hands, warning them to step carefully over the brushcutter and chainsaw. Then he took a squat bottle of brandy from his glove box and handed it to Gillian.

'For medicinal purposes,' he said with a wink. 'Enjoy.' He turned to Emily. 'Would you like to ride in the cab? I think your rooster would find it more comfortable.'

His request was met by a chorus of 'Ooooh's' from the older ladies.

He opened the door and Emily tried to sit in a dignified way without bumping the tall plumage on her head.

Andrew set his sensual mouth in a determined line. 'I bet I'll remember where I've seen you before this race day's done.'

'I bet you won't,' said Emily. 'You've never seen me before in your life.'

He cast her a cheeky look. 'Do you like racing?'

'Not particularly,' she said.

'Do you like horses?'

'Can't stand them. They terrify me.'

Andrew nodded and smiled.

'A shame. I'm looking for someone to take me round the park on horseback to show me places I can't get to with the four-wheel drive. I'm on a project to map weeds and water quality. We're looking for a team of mountain cattlemen to help us reintroduce periodic grazing to the park as a management tool. I thought I'd found the right person this morning up on the mountain. But that little bird flew away too fast for me to talk to her.'

Emily's mouth dropped open, speechless.

In the Community Club, Andrew handed Emily a beer and looked up at the TV to watch the glossy Melbourne Cup thoroughbreds so fizzed with excitement they were barely being contained in the barriers.

'The nation has now stopped,' Andrew said, chinking the edge of Emily's glass with his.

'And . . . racing!' came the voice of the TV commentator. 'First away was Law Breaker, followed by Little White Lies, Self-righteous Lass and Big Misunderstanding.' As the horses gained momentum, Emily drew her eyes away from the race and saw that Andrew was looking right at her.

'I'd love you to show me your mountain,' he said, leaning to whisper the words in her ear.

The commentator's voice became frenzied. 'Swallowed Pride is making ground, then Meaningful Dialogue, Common Sense and Good Solution. But it's Instant Attraction, Instant Attraction making a bolt to the lead.'

The women were clutching each other and screaming, their fascinators creating a sea of vivid colour and movement as the commentator roared out the final yards of the race.

'It's Love Conquers All! Love Conquers All is the winner of the Melbourne Cup!'

And in the flurry of race-day fever, Emily felt the arms of the ranger around her, and she was lifted into the air like a bird in flight.

Preserves

'More slowly, Caroline! Slower!' Hillary Beechworth stooped and peered through the jar. 'See the bubbles? You must pour more slowly.'

Caroline sat down the sticky jug of syrup on a tea towel and wiped a curl of grey hair away from her eyes with the back of her hand. She glanced at Hillary and clenched her jaw, feeling her false teeth shift along her gums.

'What would your mother say?' said Hillary as she shuffled to the stovetop and squinted at the thermometer from behind her thin spectacles. 'You'll never win a show championship with your preserves if you pour like that, young lady.'

'Hmmph,' said Caroline to the 'young lady' bit. She was far from young any more. Hillary liked to preserve time. Back to the days when Caroline wore her hair in bows. The endless ritual of summer in the kitchen. The sugary smell of boiling fruit. Hillary and Caroline's mother, teaching Caroline how to pack the jars, what mix of sugar, how to slice.

'I'm sorry. I know the mention of your mother upsets you,' said Hillary. Caroline pretended not to hear and lifted the jug to pour again. This time more slowly.

'Ah. Your dear mother. She was such a good friend and neighbour to me,' sighed Hillary as she held up a ripe peach and inspected it in the window's light. 'How we do all miss her.'

Piffle, thought Caroline.

'It's so unsettling,' said Hillary, pursing her thin lips. 'Not knowing. It's hard to credit that this is our second summer without her. God rest her soul.'

Hillary shivered a little as she thought of Marjory here in this kitchen. She always looked so neat. So very neat. And in control – even when they'd both grown so old. Marjory wore navy skirts and stiffly ironed floral shirts. When they got together to do their preserves for the annual show, she wore a crisp white apron which never seemed to stain with anything, not even when they were doing beetroot. There were the pearls, too. A strand of them, each perfectly even. Marjory always wore pearls – even in the kitchen.

Hillary shivered again.

Warmth from the summer sun radiated through the window and swam with the heat from the stove. Two hotplates hissed blue beneath the giant Fowler steriliser pot. Inside, jars filled with perfect, even slices of pears rattled as they sat in the bubble and steam of boiling water.

At the kitchen table Hillary, with gnarled old hands, expertly looped the orange rubber sealing ring over the lip of a jar. She sat it back down in the neat row of glass jars. They stood like soldiers about to march in a parade.

'I think we should do the apricots next,' Hillary said. 'Mr Hopkins left a case on the porch this morning. The season's been splendid for them. They'll certainly be fit for a blue ribbon once I've finished with them. You're younger than me, Caroline. Pop out and grab them for me, would you? We'd better get to them before the wasps do.'

Get them yourself, you old bat, thought Caroline, then saw her own reflection in the French doors. She was short and plain. Her grey hair hung down over her craggy face. No wonder she had remained Miss Caroline. Miss Spinster Caroline. Old maid. Her mother had told her she was ugly. Nearly every day of her life. Ugly. When Caroline was sixteen, she had heard Hillary whispering over a pot of steaming tomatoes.

'Is Caroline simple?' Hillary had asked. And Caroline's mother had said yes. On the back verandah Caroline looked at Hillary's fruit hanging from the greengage tree. Bees and flies buzzed through leafy green. She stepped onto the gravel path and reached up to feel the fruit between her thumb and fingers. Gently, so as not to bruise.

Not long now, she thought. Perfect for preserves. She

turned back towards the crate of apricots and lugged the wooden box inside.

'Careful, dear!' Hillary cleared a space on the bench top and waited for Caroline to put the box down. 'God's gift,' Hillary said, running her fingers over the soft fuzz of rounded fruit.

As she began to halve the apricots and put the dark kernels into an enamel bowl, she hummed.

Caroline measured out the sugar. Three pounds.

'Your mother holds the record, you know. Thirty-five years as the winner of the apricot conserve section. Thirty-five years. We shall enter together, Caroline, you and me. And we shall win. In honour of your mother.'

Caroline smiled dully and began to tip steaming water over a jangly collection of silver Fowler lids.

When she turned she looked across at Hillary's glass cabinet through the doors of the sitting room. Inside hung an array of red ribbons. Not a single slash of blue hung there amongst the ribbons and rosettes.

Hillary always came second to Caroline's mother.

Caroline smiled again.

'Oh! The pears are done! Lift them out would you, Caroline?' Caroline took the tongs and lifted the jars onto a breadboard.

'Glorious,' said Hillary from where she stood cutting apricots. 'It brings me to tears that your mother isn't here to see them. Oh my.' She wiped the corner of her eye with her apron. 'Fancy. Your mother missing. Still missing after nearly two years.' *Fancy*, thought Caroline.

Hillary pictured the policemen on her doorstep. One in a sharp uniform, the other in a sagging fawn coat. In her living room as they sipped on tea, she imagined them eyeing her second-place ribbons with suspicion.

'So you say she often went blackberrying this time of year?'

'Yes,' said Hillary, sitting with her back straight, 'at the river.'

'The river?' said the second policeman.

'Why, yes,' she said. 'It runs at the base of our gardens. She went down there every year. For jam. The berries. She was getting frail, you know. She could've slipped.'

'Slipped?' said the policeman who still wore his hat. She wished he'd taken it off inside. It was the polite thing to do. She raised a handkerchief to her mouth.

'Yes. Slipped. And fallen in.' That's what the locals now believed. That Marjory had slipped and fallen in the river and the thunderstorm of torrential rain that had tumbled from the skies that night had carried her body away.

———◆———

Today in the kitchen, Hillary removed her glasses and wiped her eyes. The constant sound of the gas stovetop and the rattling jars was making her tired. It had been a long day. Pears, peaches, apricots, tomatoes and, at last, the onions. The rhubarb could wait until tomorrow. She rubbed at her eyes again.

'How's that solution coming along for the onions, Caroline?' Caroline stirred the vinegar, sugar and cloves, breathing in the rich smell. She dipped her finger in the solution without Hillary seeing and placed a drop on her tongue. Bittersweet.

When Hillary at last ushered Caroline out, the sun was sinking low in the sky. Caroline walked towards the shadowy house next door. Her mother's house. Her house now. She went in through the back door. Creaking. She turned on the kitchen light and ran her hand along the bench tops.

What to eat? She went to the pantry. Inside stood lines of jars containing the richness of summers past. All perfectly packed by her mother's hands. There were bread and butter cucumbers, reds, greens and yellows of pickles, sauces and chutneys. Tall jars of Scotch broth and mulligatawny soup. Short squat jars of pickled eggs. Slender jars of beans, asparagus and baby carrots. Neat and tidy. Each vegetable or fruit the same size as the other.

With aching bones Caroline stepped up on the kitchen stool and reached to pull out a jar from the shelf containing the meats. Her hand clasped a squat Vacola bottle.

She held it to the light. In the murky golden pickling solution, pressed against the glass, was the face of a woman. No skull. Just skin. At the base of the jar, curled around in a perfect spiral, was a string of pearls.

'Hello, Mother,' said Caroline as she placed it carefully back in its row. Next to it, in another jar, her mother's hand waved at her through golden liquid and glass, her wedding ring catching the light from the kitchen in a sparkle. Caroline waved back and picked up a jar from the same row. It was a jar of what could have been mistaken for potted beef. Then she gathered up a box of rat poison. Perhaps Hillary would like to join her for dinner. She shut the door, stepped down from the stool and sighed with pleasure. She loved the perfect sound of a seal being broken and air rushing in as she stuck a knife under the lid.

Grandma's Gift

The other girls had been excessively envious of Edna, my grandmother. Even today, the ones who are left still whisper to each other. They shuffle their old bones into my grandmother's house, which always seems to be filled with sunshine and bright flowering geraniums.

The women sit on chintz-covered chairs for their game of bridge and eye Grandma with suspicion. Their cracked old lips, painted with lipstick, sip at gin and tonics. A slice of lemon, a 'chink' of ice on crystal and a little small talk. The women sit straight-backed, bristling with curiosity.

Grandma once told me how the other girls had swished in their white dresses and giggled on the lawn at her eighteenth birthday party, their downcast eyes looking out from beneath the brims of shady straw hats, in a charade of giggles and pouts.

The would-be actresses were playing to the most handsome soldier in the district, Archie Heathcote. He was not just tall and very handsome in a country way, but he also possessed a kind and gentle soul. He had the gift of calming other souls, whether they belonged to crusty old gentlemen or the flighty young horses Archie would break in for the army. Everyone knew he was the catch of the district, but even the prettiest and smartest girls didn't stand a chance. Not while Grandma was around.

'He was a dish, your grandfather,' she would say to me with a satisfied smile. And I would curl my legs up on the couch and hope she would tell me her story again.

His eyes had scanned all the girls at the party, but it was Edna who captured his gaze. She wasn't slim or tall or particularly outgoing. She had a gift – if you could call it that. Edna's mother had first noticed it when Edna was a girl, and was made to take tea with Mrs Brightling, who had called in to pass away another sweltering afternoon.

———————◆◆———————

Edna hated taking tea, especially with Mrs Brightling, who always took great pleasure in commenting on Edna's tomboy nature. Edna loathed nibbling politely on cucumber sandwiches and chitchatting about the weather. She preferred to roll on the springy green buffalo grass in the shade of the massive red gum with the sheepdogs, or wade in the billabong with mutton on string, fishing for yabbies. She was happiest of all in the dusty sheep yards or on a sweating stock pony tailing a mob.

Sitting bolt upright on the couch, Edna felt a hot trickle of sweat run down her spine. Her angry gaze fixed on her milky tea. And there and then, at tea with Mrs Brightling, Edna created her first storm in her teacup. Little waves splashed wildly against the floral-print cup, dark clouds hovered over its rim and torrential rain fell into the milky turbulent ocean. Bolts of lightning flashed into the cup's depths followed by low rumbles of thunder.

The cup and saucer shuddered in Edna's small hand and made rattling noises. Edna's eyes were fixed on her mini storm and her young cheeks flushed red. Her mother delivered a stinging glance at her daughter and her sisters stifled giggles.

Edna felt her mother's gaze, blinked, and the waters of her milky tea calmed.

'Edna, darling, why don't you go and water your flower bed? It's awfully hot,' her mother diplomatically suggested.

Later, her mother had sighed and said that Mrs Brightling had luckily mistook the thunder for Edna's rumbling stomach and the shaking of her cup as 'nerves'. But the event could well have caused great embarrassment and even distress to poor Mrs Brightling.

'No more storms in tea cups, Edna!' her mother had decreed.

So, instead of storms in tea cups, Edna took to flying. She would leave her body in the bed, so her mother would not notice her gone, and take to the night skies.

'It was how I won your grandfather's heart,' she would say to me.

On the night of her eighteenth birthday party she lay on her back in a streak of moonlight and closed her eyes. She felt herself lift from the weight of her body, and through the window she flew. Up towards stars, over the top of the giant red gum. She would touch her fingertips on the sleek gum leaves that shone in the moonlight and smile. Lingering from the pleasure and sensuality of those cool, rich-smelling leaves. But this night she had a plan. She was flying beyond town to Heathcote's property, Lal Lal, where she would touch his heart in his sleep.

She could see the shine of the fence wire as she whisked away above the dirt road. She was soon over the wide street of the town, then over the dully shining corrugated iron of the huge sleepy verandah that hugged the large hotel. A stray dog in the main street was the only living creature to sense her pass. The hungry thing looked up to the night sky and barked uncertainly.

She flew above the road to the south, faster now. Her cheeks red, yet cool from the pleasure of the rushing night air. She could see his family homestead. Soon she was there, hovering above Archie. He was on the bed. Short dark hair, freshly cut. Head thrown back in sleep, limbs twisted in sheets. She noticed his army kit bag packed ready to go. A frown passed over his brow but it lifted as he felt her presence. She tilted her head to the side with a gentle smile as she took in his beauty, softness and strength, sprawled out in sleep.

Edna stretched out a cool fingertip and traced a path of love over his brow, his eyelids and mouth. Her gentle finger glided over soft male skin and coarse male hair. First, his shaven chin, then over his neck and chest. He stirred a little and she breathed in the smell of him and the love of him. Then she was gone. Back across the skies and the outstretched arms of the red gum to her bed.

'He rode like a man possessed to our verandah the next day,' my grandmother delighted in telling me.

'I could see his saddle bags were full. He was off to war.' The horse's sides heaved, and froth from sweat gathered along the line of the breastplate and girth.

Archie swung a lithe leg over the horse, landing polished brown army boots on the gravel. He urged my great-grandmother to allow him a word with her youngest daughter. Open-mouthed, the sisters watched as he took Edna's arm and led her across the lawn to the shade of the red gum.

He told her of a dream he'd had the previous night and how he must have her consent to be his wife before he left for Europe. He pressed a kiss on her lips, gently but urgently. He promised to return.

That was the day my grandmother's friends began to view her with envy and suspicion. After church the young girls would gather under the shade of the pepper trees and read out excerpts from the letters penned by their young soldiers. Edna received the most frequent and loving letters from her husband-to-be. My grandmother would convert the passion contained in the looped ink writing of my grandfather to words, and the words would bring jealous tears from the other girls.

After a while the letters to Grandma's girlfriends failed to come, or failed to be written.

'I was fortunate,' my grandmother would say mildly and with genuine sadness for her friends. During those awful war years she would fly away in the night, flying faster than the wind, over land, mountains and oceans – over entire continents.

<hr />

'Beautiful trees,' she sighed, remembering the soft greenness of Europe's treetops rushing past beneath her. There were streets of cobbles, which would shine dappled after rain. Above rooftops she flew to Archie in France. She would find him stretched asleep on a canvas bed in a row of tents in a field. She would lie next to him to ease his horror and loneliness, pressing her body against his and placing an arm across his chest. He would awake filled with her. Loving and looking only for her. Those visits kept him alive.

She had travelled to him as he lay on the big steamship, tossed by angry seas, and touched him with healing in his dreams and fever. When he finally arrived home he rode his horse right up the steps and onto the verandah, straight to her.

They decided to marry under the red gum, and filled their life together with sunshine, geraniums, children and dogs amidst the difficulties of farming. One night, after many happy years, Archie had peacefully left as he slept beside Grandma. Flying upwards and out from his tired old body.

'Don't you miss him?' I asked her one day.

'No, dear. Not at all,' she said. 'Some nights I feel him fly down to see me.

He lies with me and touches my face. I can feel him with me, always.'

The old women who sit on her couch and drink her gin can't understand. They have never been able to work out my grandmother's happiness – life should be crueller to women. Widows shouldn't feel so complete.

While I sit near them, frustrated by their jealousy and sus-picion of my grandma, I notice the cup and saucer in my hand is beginning to rattle. Small angry storm clouds are forming over my cup and I can hear the sound of thunder rumbling.

The Tractor Factor

Casey Brown couldn't help sighing a little as her housemate Suzie dragged her by her handbag into yet another noisy, buzzing city pub. Despite Casey's pretty, country-girl face, wavy chocolate hair and divine Nigella Lawsonesque body, she never did much good with the city fellas. There were always plenty of men initially interested, even though she had climbed past the age of thirty. But the moment the men swivelled around from the bar and pushed their beer nearer her to ask, 'So what do you do?', she'd feel her cheeks colour.

'I'm a semen rep,' she would mumble.

'A what?'

'A *semen* rep. I sell semen . . .' Despite adding hastily, 'For the dairy industry,' the reaction from men was always the same. They would frown, then, like a puzzled kelpie, tilt their heads quizzically to the side. 'You sell *semen?*'

Most men would then burst out laughing, saying things like, 'Classic!', 'For real?'. Or, if they were in their twenties, 'Totally random!' or 'Wicked', and slap her on the back like she was one of the boys. Then pretty legal secretary Suzie, with her straight blonde hair, stick-of-cabana figure, artificial nails and fairy voice, would sweep in and score the pick of them. Casey would mentally throw her hands in the air, swilling beer down her throat like a viking.

She was the only child of a dairy farmer. A child that was supposed to have been a boy. A child that had been raised as a boy anyway. There was no one to teach her feminine charms on the farm. Her mother wore baggy navy overalls, which exactly matched her father's, daily to the dairy. She even made a tiny pair for toddler Casey to wear when she dawdled about the concrete yards, poking at steaming pats of manure with a stick, or playing beneath the lonely pine that stood near the forcing yards, throwing pine cones into the effluent pond beyond the ringlock fence, waiting for her mother to be done with the milking.

There was a photo on the kitchen buffet at home from those days: Casey, a mini-me of her mother at six, standing outside the hay-filled barn, with her mum and dad in their matching clobber of gumboots and brace and bib. Looking, as Casey thought, for all the world like a mentally deficient family from *Green Acres*. At thirteen, Casey had tried to buck the system and came home with nail polish from the Two Dollar

Shop. Her mother had shared her dairywoman wisdom that warned 'manicures and milkings never mix', and as the polish chipped off and Casey felt the warm splatters of manure rain down from above her in the pit, she realised that maybe her mother was right.

Even though Casey had loved the cows, and her dad's rough red-coated sheepdog, Massey, who sported droobles of matted fur behind his soft ears, she had been desperately lonely as a child. In her bedroom she had lost herself in books. Books that expanded her world and broadened her mind. History books, travel books, essays and, for rainy days, her mum's Mills & Boon. Casey longed to find herself in the pages of those romances. To walk, talk and dress like the heroines who stood on the precipice of being rescued by some incredible man.

So when Casey first kissed a freckle-faced Byron Cooper behind the dunnies at the Regional Heifer Sale near Shepparton, and he'd groped her breasts like he was checking for udder mastitis, she was mightily disappointed. Later, in her twenties, there was the older neighbour's son, Liam Dennison, who'd picked her up in his Torana and taken her out to the local pub for a chicken parmigiana. Instead of complimenting her, Liam found all kinds of adjectives to describe the beauty of her father's cows. It was as if he was already planning a merger of the herds and Casey was the key to his milking empire expansion.

Over the years Casey found the dairy boys nice enough, but

as time passed, she became convinced that a dairyman would never do. A life of daily milkings would never do either. She needed a bigger life than that. Hence the move to the city and her quest. A quest that seemed to be stalling no matter how hard she tried.

As they pushed through the pub crowd Casey shouted to Suzie above the din, 'I'm looking for sophistication and intellect. But I don't reckon I'll find it here.'

'Forget those qualities for now. You have to start at the bottom and just look for someone to shag. Work your way up.' Suzie steered her strategically to the bar, placing Casey between herself and a group of young men whose long Friday lunch was merging into after-work drinks and, potentially, Saturday morning spews.

'At least I won't find a farmer in here. All dairy farmers do is talk about cows. Boring.'

'Like you do,' said Suzie.

'I do not!'

'You do. When you come home from work you always rave about the new bull or cow you've found and what embryos have travelled first-class in eskys to where. So for tonight, drop the cow talk and stick your tits out. Those blokes are looking.'

Casey glanced over at the rabble at the bar, who were, in fact, eyeing them off.

She felt like she was being hunted. She watched Suzie now as she preened herself in strategic feminine ways. Perching on a barstool like a bird, leaning forward to expose just enough cleavage. Legs crossed in a ladylike fashion yet with her skirt hoiked up to her thighs, beaming at the best beau from the bar. She had perfected the art of sensuality, stroking the straw of her drink with red bejewelled nails. Casting her head coyly to one side while look up through long lashes. Then a blonde toss of locks. Casey looked down to her own hand wrapped solidly around her pint glass and the way her feet stood squarely under each blocky hip as if she were about to start a chainsaw.

Sure, in the dairy pit back home she could chuck cups on teats with her eyes shut, and at the semen depot she could swing giant canisters of frozen semen about as if they were lemonade cans. And she knew every Holstein bloodline back to front from Canada to Germany, to Ireland and Australia and back. But did she know how to pick up a fancy city bloke? *No way.*

Casey surveyed the man standing next to them, who flashed perfectly polished teeth. His tanned, waxed chest was set off by a floral shirt. His blond-tipped funked-up hair and groovy glasses gave him an 'I'm uber cool, even though I'm getting on a bit' kind of look.

'Having a big night out after work, girls?' he said. Casey nodded. Suzie preened. Then he asked, 'So where do you work? What do you do?'

'I'm a legal secretary,' twittered Suzie. 'And she sells semen.'

'For the dairy industry,' Casey added quickly.

The man faltered for a moment then, with a huge grin on his face, said, 'You sell *semen?*'

'Yes, semen. Bull semen. And embryos. For the dairy industry.'

Should she tell him she was runner-up in the Semex Semen Seller of the Year at International Dairy Week last year? Should she say she had secured deals in genetics all over the world, including cracking it big time in the Asian market? No, she didn't think so. Instead of impressing him, she knew it would make him laugh at her more. If she *had* won semen seller of the year, she harrumphed to herself, she'd now be in Canada on a dairy genetics study tour instead of stuck here talking to *him*.

The man spun around to his mate. 'Hey, Rog,' he said, slapping him on the chest, 'this chick here sells semen.'

'For the dairy industry,' Casey added.

She sighed as she saw his mate turn to her with glinting eyes.

'You sell semen.'

'Yes. Bull semen.'

'No way!' the very drunk mate said, looking her up and down lasciviously.

Here it comes, she thought.

'So do you actually wank bulls off?'

Casey shut her eyes and smiled tiredly. A vision of her father in his seventies terry-towelling hat and overalls, which these days looked as if he had stuffed a beach ball down the front, came to her mind.

'If you can't beat them, Case,' she could hear his drawling farmer tone, 'join 'em.'

'I'd like to wank bulls off,' Casey said dryly, 'but no, my boss won't let me. The collection team use an electric anal probe instead. Shock the little swimmers out.'

'Coorrr! No way!' both men called out, impressed.

It was the same every time. At this point Casey knew she'd have to steer her conversation away from semen, otherwise things turned gross and weird with men.

'Casey Brown's my name,' she said, delivering her saving line and acting all bloky and beery. 'I'm actually named after a tractor.' This provided them with even more mirth. 'Yep. Named after the 1978 Case 885 David Brown tractor. Dad's a bit of a tractor tragic. It's genetic.'

'Yeah?' said Mr Hair-funk.

She leant her elbows on the bar, just as she'd done for the past two years of Friday night drinks in the city, not caring if the blokes were listening any more. 'You see, David Brown Tractors became affiliates with Case International in 1972, so by the time I was born in '78 Dad had a brand-new Case David Brown tractor and a baby girl instead of a boy. When he came into the hospital and told Mum he wanted to name me after a tractor, she was all for it.' Another sip of beer for timing effect.

'You see, before she married Dad, Mum's name was Alice Charmers.' She wiped the back of hand across her mouth, dragging beer with it just to let them know that she was definitely one of the boys. The city men never got that bit. The bit about Alice Charmers. But it was true. It was the reason her mum and dad had got together in the first place – Casey's dad loved all tractors, including the elegant long-chassis Allis Chalmers tractor.

The moment Alice Charmers, the daughter of a diesel mechanic, met David Brown the dairy farmer, the tractor-factor connection had sparked between them. The love engine had cranked over, roared then settled down to idle well ever since, as all good diesels do. Casey always cringed when her mother retold the story.

'Your father said to me, "If I show you my power take off, will you show me your grease nipples?"' Then Alice Brown (nee Charmers) would giggle wickedly and her pink cheeks would turn pinker, recalling the day as if it were only last week.

'I'm third in line with the tractor names,' Casey said to her line-up of bar flies. 'It's a dynasty thing. My grandfather was named Fergus Brown after the first David Brown/Ferguson tractor in '36. Dad came along in '56 and so they named him David after their new David Brown 25D. And here's me . . . Case Brown if I was a boy, but I turned out a girl so I got the extra Y – if you'll pardon the pun. Casey Davida Brown. Oh, we Browns are big on the tractor factor.'

The men laughed again but inside Casey felt herself cry. Even if she scored the sophisticated, intellectual man of her dreams, how could she ever take them home and be taken seriously?

Before newcomers even got to the Browns' little weather-board farm house on the windswept and treeless soldier settlement block, Casey knew her family would appear a bit kooky. The oddness started at the gates leading into the farm, where a replica model of an Allis Chalmers served as a mail-box. Things seemed normal enough when driving past the electric fences, irrigation channels and black and white milkers grazing the green pasture, until you arrived at the house. Her dad had painted the house the exact same orange and white as the immaculate '78 Case David Brown tractor that was parked in pride of place in the skillion shed next door. On the front lawn, tractor windmills spun in technicolour whirls above gnomes driving tractors, and on the doormat a green tractor cartoon shouted, 'Come in if you think my tractor's sexy!'

Casey imagined her father greeting Mr Accountant, Mr Property Developer or Mr Barrister at the door wearing his favourite T-shirt, the one her mother had bought him last Christmas. Emblazoned across her father's XXL chest would be the words: 'I like my girls like I like my tractor . . . dirty with a big set of front weights.' Next he would usher them in to meet Alice Brown (nee Charmers) who, with a beaming smile and bright red cheeks to match her hair, would offer them a cup of tea in a tractor mug, poured from a tractor teapot sporting a tractor tea cosy, and stirred by a tractor spoon that came with the tractor creamer and matching sugar bowl. Above them the tractor clock would tick towards the end of Casey's short-lived relationship as her father told one bad joke after the next . . . about tractors.

Then there'd be the hurdle of getting the imagined visiting boyfriend through the night. Casey's bedroom was right next door to the calf shed. There the poddys bellowed for their mums or a feed, or both, around the clock, and poured liquid dung out their tiny puckered orifices, the stench of which seeped through the paintsealed windows next to Casey's single bed. She imagined having to encourage her groggy new lover to get out of bed (or at least out of the trundle bed beside her bed) at five for the Sunday morning milking. A very disagreeable situation when Mr Barrister, Mr Accountant or Mr Property Developer was used to sleeping in till ten on Sundays, reading the weekend papers and heading to a cafe cluster in a trendy inner-city suburb for a brunch of eggs Benedict.

Casey sighed.

'Well, nice to meet you,' she said to Mr Faux-blondie at the pub, 'but I've got a big day tomorrow watching the judging for Cow of the Year at the City Showgrounds.'

This set the men spluttering again as they echoed, 'Cow of the Year! You *are* joking, right?'

She turned to Suzie.

'I'm getting a cab home.'

'But . . .'

As Casey pushed through the crowd she heard the men say to Suzie, 'Is your friend for real? She's so *funny*!'

At home in her flat, Casey pulled on the cow-print PJs her mum had sent her and pulled the doona over her head. A doona her mother had bought her . . . one with cows on it. 'So you don't miss the girls too much,' she had written on the card.

As she drifted off to sleep Casey wondered when something was going to happen in her life. When would the world turn and her engine be cranked over by love? She scrunched her eyes tight and with as much determination as Dorothy clacking her bejewelled red slippers, said, 'Please make it be tomorrow. Please make it be tomorrow.'

———•———

'Maybe I should head back to the country,' Casey said to Suzie the next morning as she watched the parade of dairy cows sail like a fleet of ships onto the imitation grass of the indoor show ring. 'People in the city don't "get" me.'

Suzie looked at her over a fuzz of pink fairy floss, oblivious to the stares she was attracting in her tiny pink shorts and fake cowgirl boots of the same hot pink, worn in honour of Casey's country culture. Suzie was mightily hungover and a bit stiff in her hips from her one-night stand.

'What do you mean people don't get you? No one gets you. I don't get you.'

'What's not to get?' Casey said, irritated now. Suzie waved her fairy floss to encompass the scene before her.

'This! This cow biz. It's freaky.'

'Freaky? This is where your milk comes from. It's a multi-million-dollar industry. And incredibly complex.'

'It's weird. The people are weird. You're weird. Don't get me wrong, Casey, you're nice and everything, but . . . weird. I mean, look at you. It's your day off and here we are looking at bloody cows! You wouldn't catch me reading up on the law on the weekend, unless it was in bed with the senior partner.'

'Yes, but I should be married with children, shouldn't I? I'm getting old! Almost past it for breeding —' she stopped mid-sentence as she surveyed the third cow in the line up. 'I like number eleven. Showtime bloodlines, by the look, and perfect udder and teats. Nice bone too. But really, Suze, there are no men here for me.'

'No men! A city this size, there are men *everywhere*. And you're not old.'

'Easy for you to say. You're still in your twenties.'

'But what are you looking for? You told me the last place you want to be is back home on your farm pulling tits twice a day for the rest of your life. But you don't want what's out there in the pubs, and you don't want what's here.' Suzie was waving her fairy floss to emphasise her point.

Casey shook her head.

'Oh, I don't know. Can we just not talk about it? They're about to judge the interbreed to decide Cow of the Year.'

Suzie rolled her eyes and stifled a sick burp as Casey turned to devour the sight of a delicious caramel and cream Guernsey as she paraded behind a leggy Holstein.

'She's a magnificent breed type,' Casey said.

Suzie ran her eyes over the parade of cattle handlers who, unlike the cows, varied greatly in shape and size, but were all dressed in the same uniform of white shirt and white trousers.

'Someone should tell them if you wear all white, you ought to wear a beige g-string underneath. You can see their undies,' Suzie whispered loudly. 'It's disgusting.'

'Shush!'

'God, Casey! This is so boring. Can we go?'

'*Shush!*'

The cows and handlers came nearer to the girls, who had taken front-row positions at the ring to watch the cows battle it out.

'Christ! Look at the size of those tits!' Suzie almost screeched. Casey was well used to the appearance of show cows, but it did make her eyes water seeing the pink skin over the Holstein's udder stretched taut like a drum. Underneath, fat veins ran in ridges over the udder surface and the teats stuck out at seemingly unnatural angles, spraying fine jets of white milk onto the plastic imitation-grass carpet. The cow had to swing her hind legs out around her bulging udder as she walked. The handler, a tubby man with sideburns, tugged gently on the cow's shiny leather halter to make her stand correctly in the line-up before the judge.

Next lumbered the Brown Swiss, her pretty dark eyes looking calmly at the mass of people sitting high in the stands. Casey knew her as the veteran champion cow, Donnyvale Talula Kitty. Daughter of Riversbend Sunset Glimmer and sired by Fairbrook Starfizz Northernlights. The queen of the show ring. The cow put her ears forward and walked as elegantly as she could, despite her bulging udder. A fur stole would not have looked out of place on the ladylike creature. Casey felt a buzz run through the crowd as Kitty took her position next to the Holstein.

'Check out the bag on her! She's bound to win best vessel too!' Casey said, enraptured by the animal.

With her eyes so firmly on the cow it took her a while to realise Suzie was elbowing her in the ribs.

'What?' she hissed.

'Check out the guy with the brown cow.'

'The Brown Swiss.'

'What?'

'She's a Brown Swiss and she's magnificent.'

'No! Check out the handler. He's a bit of all right.'

Casey tore her eyes away from the cow and saw the youngish man was not too shabby.

'He does have nice arms.'

'And a nice cleft,' Suzie whispered.

'Huh?'

Suzie indicated a vertical line on her chin with a ruby-red nail. 'Cleft. *Sexy.*'

Casey nodded, just as a Jersey cow with an impossibly golden coat, exquisite dark points and a gleaming black nose drifted into the place beside the Brown Swiss. The handler, a bald man with silver-rimmed glasses, looked as red as a beetroot from the stress of the occasion. The judge, distinguished in tweed with an overdone pants crease, stepped forward and in a surprisingly loud voice boomed, 'Could handler Ken Worth with Brown Swiss number seven step forward, please.'

Casey's jaw dropped.

'Oh my God.'

'What?' Suzie asked.

'Give me the program!' She snatched the show schedule from Suzie's grasp and began to run her index finger down the list of handlers.

And there it was in black and white in the Brown Swiss section. Ken Worth! She gasped.

'What?'

'Him . . . that man. His name is *Ken Worth*!'

'So?'

'It's a truck name. A Kenworth is a truck.'

'So?'

'It's that whole name connection! It's a sign! It's a meant-to-be kind of thing.' Casey grabbed at Suzie's arm, 'We have to meet him.'

'But he's a tit puller.'

'But he's named after a truck.'

'Yes. A truck, Casey. Not a tractor. That's a tractor-truck factor not a tractor-tractor factor. Still, he could do for a truck-fuck.'

'You're taking the piss out of me. You always take the piss.'

Suzie looked at her with a crinkled-up nose as if she'd just smelt something horrible. Casey, normally so placid, felt her cheeks burn with fury.

'I'm tired of it, Suzie. Since when is it a crime to be passionate about something? What's the harm in being passionate about cows? These girls supply not just us with milk, but the whole world. I know the dairy industry is flawed and we have changes to make. Many changes, but —'

'Oh, for God's sake, Casey. You're just uptight because you need a root. Same as those poor cows you deal with who only ever see a canister instead of a real bull. Really!'

Casey shook her head sadly. 'I know you've tried, Suzie, but it's useless. *I'm* useless. At least, I am around here. I've suddenly realised I've been ashamed of a way of life, and I shouldn't be. I've been ashamed of my own mum and dad. But mostly, I've been ashamed of *myself*.'

'Look, this isn't *Dr Phil*. It's a cow show. Can you save your epiphanies for the pub, please? I need the hair of the dog . . . now. Let's go. Tonight, I promise, we'll find you a fella.'

'No, Suzie. Tonight I'm packing. I'm going home. Home to milk cows with my mum and dad. And if it means wearing overalls for the rest of my life and living alone, then I don't care. At least I'll be understood . . . part of my own herd.' As Casey delivered her tirade in frenzied whispers she was suddenly surprised by a scream from the show ring. Followed by shouts. Then cows scattered everywhere. At the epicenter of the ruckus was Mr Bald Handler. With blind fury he'd leapt on Ken Worth's back and was pummelling him from behind.

'Get that spineless cheating mongrel!' a woman handler with a bad yellow perm screamed. Ken Worth was fast falling backwards, taking his regal cow with him. His attacker, attached to his back, was roaring like an enraged lion.

'Get off me!' Ken Worth shouted.

Men rushed to drag the bald man from Ken. His Brown Swiss, now in a state of panic, swung her broad body around, knocking over a bench seat full of showgoers. Photographers from the rural papers leapt into the ring, snapping pictures. Flashes lit up the pavilion, startling the cattle even more. The crowd rumbled with shock as more handlers joined in the punch-up. Casey watched in disbelief while Suzie squealed with delight, shouting, 'Bring it on, cowboys!'

There was a momentary lull when the two men were at last separated. But it was short-lived. Bald Man broke free of his restrainers with a *Mad Max* roar and hurled himself at Ken Worth. The impact was solid. It sent the large man flying. Flying towards Casey.

On impact, Casey discovered Ken Worth was a beefy man, not all of it muscle. He knocked the air from her lungs, but not before she'd taken in the rather unpleasant scent of his armpits. Her last thought before she hit the deck was, *I'm being knocked over by a Ken Worth!* As her head hit the concrete of the dairy pavilion, Casey Brown was knocked out cold.

In the hospital Casey felt the pain of her headache drag her in and out of the here and now. Through blurred vision she could just make out the radiant frizz of her mother's halo of deep-red curly hair and the shining, smiling round face of her dad.

'Back again, Case,' he said, gently laying huge hands, ultra soft and soothing from all those years of applying udder cream to his cows' teats, on her arms.

'We were worried about you. Not like you to sleep in, pet,' her mum was saying. 'I'll go fetch the doctor and he can give you the once-over.' She winked when she said it.

Casey tried to think, but all she could remember was Suzie in pink turning red from the lecture Casey had given her. And her resolve to move back home to the farm.

'What happened? Was I hit by a truck?'

Her dad laughed softly. 'Of sorts.'

He held up a newspaper with a picture of her on an

ambulance trolley being wheeled out from the pavilion as a disturbed Guernsey show cow looked on.

'Ken Worth. Not a nice man by all accounts. American. But you and he made the front page.'

Woman Injured in Teat Cheat's Tussle! the headline shouted.

'Performance-enhancing drugs for cows had caused the row.' Her dad paraphrased the article in his slow drawl. 'Mr Worth had been accused by his dairy industry peers of using a drug from the United States to artificially enhance the size and appearance of an udder, by injecting a foam into the teats. Mr Worth was left lying in the dust after being punched in the face and a woman was taken to hospital, unconscious, after being knocked over in the brawl. The woman remains in a stable condition but has not yet regained consciousness.

'That would be you,' her father added. 'But clearly you've regained consciousness now.' He turned the page and there was a picture of Ken Worth with his broken glasses and his head in his hands.

Casey sighed. She'd thought he was going to be the one. The man to change her life's path.

Next thing, she felt the nausea rise and suddenly her mother was back in the room reaching for a pudding bowl from the meal tray that her father had clearly polished off earlier.

As Casey had her face in the bowl dry retching until her

whole body ached, she wondered if her life could get any more tragic.

'I'm sorry, Mum. I'm sorry, Dad. I've been a terrible daughter to you,' she sobbed.

'Nooo,' soothed her mother. 'We're so proud of you, Case.'

'But I haven't been proud of you. I'm so sorry. I've been judgemental and awful. I want to come home. I want to help you and Dad on the farm.'

'My! You did get a bump on the head,' her dad said, patting her arm. 'Don't you get yourself upset, dear. It does no good. Now where's that doctor?'

Casey could hear the emotion choke his words. She knew it would make their hearts soar if she came back home, and she knew it would make her own heart sing to be back home with the cows, and the paddocks and the tractors.

'I decided to I wanted to come home *before* I was hit by Ken Worth.' Then, the small family of three gathered for a hug and Casey felt herself wrapped in the bigness and softness of her parents' love. The magic moment was broken when in breezed the doctor. But then, Casey felt another magic moment begin.

'Ah, she's come round then,' he sang in a divine Irish accent. 'Feeling better now you've done the up-chuck? I could hear you ten wards away.'

Casey blushed and tried to plump her hair self-consciously.

'Now let me take a look at you,' he said, reaching for the

stethoscope that hung about his neck. 'It's nice that you could join us, Casey. You had your ma and da a tad worried.'

He shone a light in her eyes and as he did, Casey's vision came in and out of focus on his patterned tie.

'Are they cows?'

The doctor held up his tie.

'Hem, yes. Indeed they are cows.'

'Am I dreaming?'

Her parents laughed.

'No, sweet,' her mother soothed. 'Your good doctor here grew up on a dairy farm.'

'Correct!' the doctor said. 'I'm from a wee farm in Killarney in County Kerry. Da's still there, milking morning and night. Cows, cows, cows. Ma sent me the tie so I wouldn't miss the girls too much.'

Casey's eyes roamed over the doctor's face. He had reddish-blond hair and lively light-blue eyes that creased at the corners. His skin was pale and freckled and he was a little on the podgy side, but Casey thought he looked almost edible. Gorgeous, in fact. Like a marshmallow biscuit.

'You know you've been out cold for three days,' he went on cheerfully as he inspected her charts. He said 'three' as if it were 'tree', and Casey felt a smile grow deep inside her despite her pounding head.

Much to her amazement, the doctor then hitched one of his buttocks up onto the hospital bed and sat there as if he were Suzie lobbing into her bedroom for a chat. Beneath his blue jeans Casey noticed Holstein-print socks.

'Now excuse me, Casey, but I've got one for your da. It's my turn.'

'Pardon?'

'A joke. We've been going round for round since you first came in here, haven't we, David?'

She looked over to her parents, who were beaming at the doctor.

'Now you just ignore us and rest up,' he said as he lay his hand on Casey's arm. Casey could feel a gentle healing energy pass from his palm to her skin. She wanted him to keep touching her, but instead he removed his hand and turned to face her father.

'Now, David, have you heard the one about the tractor fanatic who one day decided to sell his superb collection of vintage tractors so that he could fulfill his lifelong dream of joining the fire brigade?'

'No,' Casey's father said, shuffling his chair closer, 'I haven't heard that one.'

'On his first fireman job,' the doctor said in his Irish accent, 'there was a huge building on fire. It was massive! People inside screaming, flames shooting from the windows. A terrible, terrible fire. At last, when they broke down the doors, the tractor fanatic told his fellow firemen to step aside. And to their amazement, with one gigantic inhalation the tractor fanatic sucked all the smoke and air from the building. Yes! He breathed in all the air so the fire could no longer burn, thereby saving the people trapped within. He was hailed as a hero. And when the media clustered around to ask him how he did it he said, "Well, it was easy . . . I'm an ex-tractor fan." '

Casey's jaw dropped as she watched her father and mother screech with laughter. His joke was just as bad as her father's but there was something about the accent that made it uproariously funny.

She couldn't help it. She snorted. She wheezed. She laughed until she cried. Despite the pain in her skull.

'Ex-tractor fan! Ha! Ouch, it hurts to laugh. My head!' It wasn't until she stopped laughing that she saw the doctor standing by her bed looking incredulously at her, with sincerity in his eyes.

'Oh, my Lord!' he said quietly. 'There *is* a God! You're the very first young woman to *ever* laugh at my tractor jokes! Incredible. Mr Brown, I think your daughter is *amazing*! Beautiful too.' He looked at her with genuine warmth as he handed her some painkillers and a glass of water. 'All the nurses round here call me Doctor Dag. They just don't get me. But you, Casey, you get me. As do your lovely ma and da.' He beamed at them.

'Why, thank you, Doctor Deere,' Casey's father said proudly.

Casey propped herself up in bed.

'Excuse me. Did you say Doctor Dear, Dad?'

Her father nodded and her mother looked as if she was about to tell Casey she'd won Lotto.

'Doctor Dear as in "Oh dear"?' Casey asked.

'No, dear,' her mother said, moving over to the bed. 'It's Doctor Deere as in Doctor Jon Deere. As in the tried and true green and yellow tractor.'

The doctor held up his hospital pass to Casey.

'My ma insisted we leave the 'h' out of Jon so it wasn't so obvious that I was named after Da's tractor. I've been the pride of my parents but the brunt of jokes all my life. Makes one stronger, I find, having a daft name.'

Casey looked from his face to the name tag.

'Your name *is* Jon Deere?' she said almost breathlessly.

'Yes. Indeed I have a tractor factor to my life, as you do too, Miss '78 Casey 885 Brown. And what's more, my sister Mary back in Ireland sells semen just like you. For the dairy industry. She cops it from the fellas too when she goes to Dublin, just like your ma tells me you do.'

Casey almost choked on the water as she swallowed the tablets. Was she hallucinating? Was it part of the concussion?

Her mother leant over and began to plump Casey's pillows.

'It's true,' she whispered, stroking Casey's hair gently. 'His name is Jon Deere. So, why don't you ask if you can check out his three-point linkage, after his rounds, if you show him your gear box? He's *very* cute!'

'*Mum!*' Casey tried to shout in a whisper. Her mum beamed

wickedness, while both Jon Deere and her father pretended not to hear.

Later that night, Casey Brown shut her eyes in her hospital bed but couldn't sleep for excitement. First there was the scent of red roses from her bedside, soothing her and thrilling her all at once. Doctor Jon Deere had dropped them in after his last round. Then there was the romantic replay she recalled over and over in her mind. A classic Mills & Boon scene, when Doctor Deere had extended an invitation for her to have dinner with him the moment she felt better. The way he'd touched her hand again, looking deep into her eyes, and how the sparks between them had flown. How he'd asked, 'Is it too soon to ask to kiss you?' And she had shaken her head, her thick dark hair, freshly but gingerly washed that afternoon by her mother, actually feeling like 'locks'.

Tonight as she lay back to dream, she could see her life before her, overflowing. A life of milk and honey. Helping Doctor Jon in his newly painted surgery in the heart of her hometown. The two of them walking hand-in-hand along the laneways, bringing the cows in on hot summer afternoons when the sun lit the world golden and slanted shadows of fence posts across the green pastures. Doctor Jon standing with her dad in a field of spuds, both men in overalls, toasting the crop with a beer. Men happy with the soil beneath their gumboots and their women beside them. Jon Deere kissing her in the tractor shed.

Finally, before she drifted off to sleep, Casey saw them pushing prams along the gravel drive, with little mini Deeres nestled inside, wrapped in tractor-print baby blankets. She saw it with such a blissful clarity that she could feel it unfolding already. The tractor-factor dynasty living on. The engine of love sparking, then revving, then gently slowing to a comfortable idle, for the rest of time.

Mr Foosheng's Carpet

The carpet is so plush it's like my toes are sinking into clouds. Mr Foosheng chose it because he said it was whiter than the clouds. But clouds aren't white in the city. Not outside my window, anyway, where Grollo's concrete towers rise up and up and teeter over the choppy grey of Port Phillip Bay. My husband Tony is at work with his canvas backpack slumped by his desk. He taps away at his computer, writing of taxi fares spoken in foreign tongues and travellers' pensions where the rooms are clean and cheap. After work he's leaving for Nepal. He and his canvas bag, heading above the clouds for his next assignment. He has a deadline to meet. The new edition of the book will be full and fat with the promise of destinations.

'Of course I'm staying home this time,' I said to Tony this morning as steel doors slid shut across his face and the lift moved silently down. Perhaps he's still cross. I know Tony would've preferred parquet tiling in natural wood, but Mr Foosheng wouldn't have it.

'Acrylics are purer,' Mr Foosheng had said as he signed the cheque with his Parker Sonnet lacquer pen. He'd touched my hand and Tony had looked away. 'I want you to have rich carpet so you feel like you are dancing on the clouds.' Mr Foosheng talks in whispers.

I am dancing now on cloud carpet, over to our DeLonghi four-slice toaster. Mr Foosheng saw it in a glossy weekend magazine and liked how it gleamed. It's nice to have a nice toaster. When we lived in Hong Kong, me and Tony, we didn't have a toaster. We grilled thick chunks of white bread over gas and the edges burnt black. We ate our toast lying under the scraping sound of the dusty ceiling fan, spreading crumbs on our damp sheets. The air was so hot it wrapped around our skin like honey. Tiny crumbs stuck to the honey sweat and scratched us when we made love.

We first met Mr Foosheng in Hong Kong. I was doing temp work. It was a Monday when he came into the office. He held my face in his small brown hands and said, 'I have found you.' He likes to spend money on art, Mr Foosheng. On beautiful things. All day I would sit at the reception desk of his office in the high tower and answer the phone. Behind me, on the wall above my head, was a nude lady in watercolour. Mr Foosheng liked to stare at her. Later, under swinging paper lanterns, beside fortune-telling birds, Mr Foosheng walked me and Tony to a cluttered, dark restaurant. It swirled with Hong Kong heat and bitter smells. He waved his hands in the thick air and told us in his whispers that he was Buddhist.

'In my life, I have had good fortune. Now I wish to pass on my good fortune, as is the law of Buddha, and I have chosen you.' Mr Foosheng looked into my eyes and put his hand on mine.

Tony looked at his plate. Beneath the table he rubbed at his ring finger. Under the band of gold, in the tiny crevices of pale skin, bacteria thrived in wet heat. The red rash made him frown, so Tony slipped his ring into his pocket. Mr Foosheng frowned too and held Tony's hand to look closely at the rash. From his pocket he pulled out an ointment and instructed Tony to rub it on 'to give relief'. He's very kind that way, Mr Foosheng.

Mum and Dad back in Castlemaine call Mr Foosheng my 'benefactor'. Their friends would ask with nasally sarcasm, 'But what does he really want?', and Mum and Dad would say, 'Oh, he's a Buddhist, you know. He just wants to hand the good fortune on to her.' Mum and Dad have never met Mr Foosheng, but they like him. He sent me a Pajero once, all the way from Hong Kong, and I gave it to them. There's more use for a Pajero in Castlemaine than here. Besides, there was nowhere to park it at the apartments. Mr Foosheng likes me to drive him with the top down in the BMW, although he always holds onto his hair and combs it down with ointment after we've arrived. There is a pool and a gym here and we, as residents, can use them when we like. Tony has never used them though, the pool or the gym. At the auction, when the bidding on the apartment went over $560 000, Mr Foosheng whispered to me, 'The gym and pool, as extra, make it worth it. Our bodies are our temples in which Buddha dwells. You must use these things to keep your temple clean and in health.'

Tony hates gym exercise. He prefers to climb mountains with a sherpa at his heels. But I have plenty of time for the gym. When my friends come to my apartment and say, 'Don't you get bored?' I say, 'Why should I work? Not me. I'm not going to work like everybody else does.'

Today is Tuesday and I normally go rollerblading along the path beside the bay. I go in the lunch hour when the Grollo construction workers sit at the kiosk in plastic yellow chairs. From behind dark glasses, they watch me roll by. They seem to like my long limbs and dark tan and my blonde hair flying behind. They worship my temple with their eyes. Today, though, I won't go to the beachside. Mr Foosheng's stretch limo from the airport will be here soon. I will make him his drink from the juicing machine he gave me. Mr Foosheng says carrot juice is good for my skin. Alcohol is very bad. Mr Foosheng never drinks, but sometimes he smokes those fat cigars and says, 'Like John Wayne.' He smiles with tiny gold and black teeth.

Soon I hear the lift doors slide open and a key in the door.

Mr Foosheng has his own key. And there he is, standing on the clouds in the living room looking at me. Here is my Buddha, here is my benefactor, in an uncrushable Armani suit.

'You must be tired from your long flight, Mr Foosheng,' I say. He smiles at me and I say, 'You have new glasses, Mr Foosheng. I love the gold frames. They make you look so smart.'

I see he has new teeth too. New American teeth. But I think it may be impolite to mention them, so I offer him a seat on the white Moran leather couch. He sits, like Monkey on a cloud, and pats the cushion next to him. His lips are a strange mottled brown, like two thin slugs lying side by side. When his mouth opens to whisper I can see the insides of the slugs. Rich purple, each connected by white strings like wet glue, which stretch and break as he whispers to me about the electronic blinds. He presses the button and Port Phillip Bay slides behind the white stretch of canvas. The room is cool and dark, but still so white. Mr Foosheng is cool and dark on the white-cloud couch. I feel his hands on my skin. They are small brown hands with purple palms. His fingers inside me feel like bigger slugs than his small lip-slugs.

'But you are a Buddhist, Mr Foohsheng,' I breathe, the leather couch squelching under my thighs as we slide to the carpet, but he says nothing. He just makes small noises in his throat as he moves and I can see his gold glasses and his gold rings shine in the white dark. Now Mr Foosheng is sliding his penis into me. Mr Foosheng's penis is small and brown, like a cigar, and I think of Monica Lewinsky and Bill Clinton. Not John Wayne. The plush carpet feels so soft on my back. I think of Tony looking out the window of the plane. An oval of clouds is his view. And there I am, sprawled out on those clouds with Mr Foosheng pumping his fortune into me. Me, the temple. Above the plane, above me and Mr Foosheng, above the clouds, is Buddha. Buddha sits cross-legged and watches us. His arms move graciously around in the swirling air. A perfect green jewel sits on his pale white forehead, above his dark slanted eyes. Far below him in the clouds, he watches the Benefactor humping the Beneficiary and the Fool flies on through the clouds.

When I get up from lying on the clouds, Mr Foosheng instructs me to shower in the white-tiled bathroom. Then, he takes me to Tiffany, near the casino, and buys me a perfect green jewel set in gold.

The Evolution of Sadie Smith

'I pod!' said Sadie Smith scathingly, as she snapped another pod in half and let the pale-green broad beans rattle into the chipped enamel bowl. She snatched up another bean and scowled at the recently opened parcel that sat before her on the coffee table.

'I pod? Of course *I pod*,' she said, looking down at her man-sized hands, their creases stained with the green flesh of bean pods. There were rows and rows of the buggers still to pick in the veggie garden. They had been Bryan's favourite, but she loathed them. She snorted a little so her belly wobbled beneath her floral house frock.

The bloody post office! Couldn't they get anything right? It was enough to deal with the farm, let alone the daily influx of mail that had followed Bryan's death. She had too much on her plate already without receiving a parcel that was meant for someone else. It was just another bugger-up designed to plague her. Sadie scratched angrily at her short brown curly hair and scrunched up her nose. She'd have to beg a lift to town again with bloody Beverly to sort it out. That meant an hour in the car listening to Bev's lecture on how best to face widowhood. Or her sermon about how she'd like to put the rest of the church ladies back in their boxes come Sunday. Sadie looked down at Michael, who lay at her feet twitching in his Jack Russell dream-space.

'I dunno,' she said to the dog. 'Help me out on this one, Michael.' But the dog only whimpered and galloped his little legs as if chasing a phantom rabbit.

Sadie looked again at the neatly printed address label. *S Smith, Forestdale Road, Edenville, Tasmania*. It was her address, all right, but they had the wrong Smith!

Sadie lifted up the white box that had been tucked inside the package and rattled it, but it gave her no clues. It had a neat Apple logo sticker on it. Sadie wondered why on earth anyone would need one of these iPod dooverlackies. It sounded like something from outer space.

If only she had children, they would know. They'd be teen-agers by now and they'd be able to tell her all about iPods. But Bryan didn't like children. Said he was too old to have them. Same as he didn't like women who drove.

Sadie sat the box down next to the larger package and returned to shelling the pale-green broad beans. There'd be bags and bags to freeze. What was the point anyway now that there was no Bryan to eat the leathery, bitter beans?

No Bryan. Sadie twisted her mouth to the side. She thought back to last summer, when she'd found him lying on his belly in the yard, his face ghostly white, cheek pressed into the soft mound of a fresh sheep turd, his eyes staring at nothing. He clutched a lump of wood in his fist and the sheepdog was still cowering under the stock-loading ramp. The sheep had remained huddled in a corner, sniffing cautiously at the hillock of man in front of them, relieved his hulking yelling form was now silent. His ticker no longer ticking.

Sadie shivered at the memory. Stock work had always stressed Bryan. And as for all that beer and pork fat, she'd told him often enough to lay off it. At least she could now have Michael inside without Bryan going off his rocker. And she could have the telly on during the day.

Sadie picked up the remote control and pressed the button. There before her flashed a woman and a man on an exercise contraption with ripples of muscle shimmering under their tanned skin. Sadie looked down at her own body. It had taken on the shape of an apple since she had married Bryan.

At the time, as a rosy-cheeked, curvy nineteen-year-old, becoming a wife had seemed like the grown-up thing to do. There were a few scraggly younger men in the district, but they didn't stand a chance with her mother, the much older Bryan, and his mother about. The Smiths often married Joneses in the district. It was the way it had always been. Or so the mothers told Sadie.

'Want to change your life?' the woman on the television said, flashing her dark beautiful eyes and tossing her glossy long hair at Sadie.

'Bugger off,' Sadie said, as she aimed the remote at her and changed channels. Up sprung a man and woman, walking hand-in-hand along a beach.

'I'm happier now than I've ever been,' said the grey-haired, pearly-toothed lady. 'Since starting Doreen Nature's Weight Loss System I've been given back my life. Do you want to change *your* life?' Sadie looked away from the woman's intense blue eyes, sighed and turned the television off.

She sat for a time in the threadbare armchair, the enamel bowl of beans on her lap, while outside the earth turned slowly, framing the sun between two bush-covered mountains.

'Well, do I?' she asked herself now in the stillness. 'Do I want to change my life?'

Bryan had said she would never change. She would always be useless. Even if she *did* want to change, how could she? Just then, as the sun dipped beneath the crown of the mountains, a beam of yellow-gold light radiated through the window. Sadie looked in wonderment as the sun's ray spotlit the parcel on the table. It was like God saying, 'Open me.' Suddenly Michael was awake and up on all-short-fours, barking at nothing, tail wagging, ears pricked. Sadie looked out the window, but there was no one. She slumped back in her chair. She remembered a story she'd once read at school about a girl opening a box. A box of troubles. What was it again? That's right, Sadie thought, it was called 'Pavlova's Box'. Or something. Opening this parcel could open up a whole world of trouble. She glanced again at the Apple sticker and was reminded of Reverend Reg's sermons in church about Adam and Eve. The trouble began with an apple. And with Eve. And here she was being offered an apple. Sadie bit her bottom lip, trying to quash the temptation that fizzed inside her.

The next morning a cracker frost met Sadie at the back porch as she dragged on her gumboots and threw Bryan's big old khaki coat over her homespun jumper and maroon tracky daks. The metal handle of the milk bucket bit cold into her palm as she trudged across the crusted frozen paddocks to the milking shed, wire-haired Michael in tow. A small mob of killers looked up from their ice-cold grazing and watched the dog and Sadie pass. Frost coated their woolly backs and their breath came as fog from their noses.

Near the shed, Mavis the cow was waiting for her breakfast. A warm steaming pat sat near her hocks, providing one dark splodge in the world of misty white. In the stalls a little black and white calf bellowed hungrily.

'All right, Poddy, all right! I'm coming,' Sadie grumbled to the impatient calf. She slung down the bucket, gave the cranky cow her tucker and dropped the pin in the head-bale to keep her anchored. She was moody, this one, and the poddy calf was a nutter, Sadie thought as she swallowed up a stool with her backside. She sat, rubbing her hands together for warmth before reaching into her pocket for the sleek silver device that trailed two white earphones on thin cords.

'Look, Mavis, you old bag. An iPod.' The cow responded by stomping her back leg and swishing her tail in bad-tempered resignation. Sadie turned to the poddy calf. 'Bet you've never seen an iPod before neither, hey, Pod? I-Pod. You-Pod.' She chuckled at her own wit.

'I know it's not meant for me, but I might as well give it a try. I'm sending it back as soon as I can get to town.'

She wondered who had ordered the glossy print brochures and books that were part of the 'Awakening Kit' that promised to 'transform her life'. The kit also had a cord to charge the iPod device which, according to the booklet, was already loaded with all the 'tools' needed for 'an awakening of consciousness'. As she'd plugged it in for an overnight charge, Sadie had vowed she would just have one tiny listen first thing, then package it all up again.

This morning she found her hands shaking more from nerves than cold as she shoved the earphones up under her beanie and squinted at the device for the 'on' switch.

'Here goes,' she said, as the iPod glowed to life.

Even the lightest touch of her forefinger caused the machine to jump to attention, scrolling through a list on the screen. Sadie watched the blinking blue line click up and down the list. She pressed an arrow button and suddenly in her ears came the sound of rain. She snorted with distaste. Here she was living in an area of thirty-four-inch rainfall, where it pissed down for much of the winter. The last thing she wanted to hear was bloody rain. What were these people thinking?

She jabbed a finger at the screen and heard the slow wash of waves over a beach. If she wanted waves, she could get a lift with Reverend Reg to the beach near one of his other parish churches. But why would she go to the beach when there was all that sand to get in your crevices and all those bloody jack-jumper ants?

She poked the iPod again and heard gongs, underlaid with hippy music. It was quite nice, Sadie thought, reaching for Mavis's teats, even though it did sound foreign. As she began to squeeze liquid threads of milk into the bucket, she wondered how rain, waves and hippy crap would 'transform her life'. Bloody tech-head townies, she thought, they didn't have a clue.

As she milked, a man began to speak in soft gentle tones. He sounded American, like one of the Muppets, and he was saying something about Deli Llamas. Deli Llamas? Bloody Americans. They were always going on about their McDonalds and the deli choices on their menus. Why did people have to start eating llamas in this country when Aussie beef and lamb were perfectly fine?

'The purpose of our life is to seek happiness,' said the man. *To seek happiness?* Sadie shook her head. Wasn't the purpose of life to work and die with bugger-all? Where was happiness when she had the whole farm and house to run by herself, which she had done anyway while Bryan was alive, with no thanks or help from him.

'Happiness comes from being present in the now,' said Muppet Man. 'It is about shutting out the sound of your own voice in your head and *being. Simply being.* Feeling the life within you.'

What? What voice in my head? This Muppet man was giving her the irrits. 'You must *listen*, for in silence you may hear the wisdom of God,' said Muppet Man.

'Silence! I'll give you silence,' said Sadie, as she jabbed the stop button and shoved the iPod in her pocket. *What a load of rot*, she heard herself think. Sadie blinked. *Was that the voice?* she heard the voice in her head say. She almost fell off her milking stool. She had never *noticed* a voice in her head before, but there it was! She listened again. *There isn't a voice in my head. You stupid woman. Shut up and get on with it.* Yes, she could hear it! It was a nasty version of Sadie, telling her she was fat, and sore, and old, and hopeless. Then Sadie noticed the voice sounded a lot like Bryan's.

Was Muppet Man right about the head voices? Maybe

she should give the iPod another go? She reached into her pocket and this time selected something called 'The Positive Life Meditation'. A woman who sounded like she was from an Indian call centre for Telstra came on saying something about the human brain.

'This meditation technology leads the listener into deep brainwave patterns to accelerate mental, emotional and spiritual growth,' soothed the Telstra lady. 'Lie back somewhere quiet and comfortable and we shall now begin.'

Sadie wondered what she was on about. As if she had time to lie about! But then some music came on, along with bird noises and waterfall sounds. Cripes, these bloody greenies and their nature. Didn't they know living out in the bush was hard bloody work and not relaxing at all? But as she milked, she pressed her forehead into the cow's warm flank, shut her eyes and listened.

She kept a steady rhythm of squeeze, squirt, squeeze, squirt and, as she did, Sadie Smith forgot the coldness of her toes. She forgot the ache in her back. She forgot the endless list of chores she had to do that day. She forgot how scared and lonely she felt. And at last the voice in her head was silent. Instead, Sadie just milked and breathed. For the first time ever she just milked, breathed and allowed the music to wash right through her.

'I can't see the point of them,' Beverly said as she dropped the Toyota back into third going down round the mountain bend. 'If you want to listen to music, you turn on the wireless.'

'But what if the cricket's on? Or what if there's music on you don't even like? With one of these things you can put the entire Tom Jones collection onto it and listen to him night and day if you want.'

'Tom Jones night and day? Well, that'd be just asking for trouble,' Beverly said, her orange lipstick-coated lips pulling down towards her chins.

'Where's the trouble in that?'

'It's Tom Jones,' hissed Beverly. 'Don't you know women take their underwear off for him and toss it at him while he's on the stage?'

Sadie giggled. 'Imagine that. If we threw our undies at him, Bev, we'd snuffocate him! I'm sure he'd love it, though. Our gigantic undies. His face.'

Bev shook her head.

'Sadie! That's disgusting! Your Bryan's not been long in the grave. You should be grieving. Not thinking of throwing your underpants about! And my underpants are not gigantic. At least not as big as yours.'

Sadie looked down to the parcel on her lap and thought for a few moments. She stared at the bushland blurring past the ute.

'Unhappiness or negativity is a disease of our planet,' she said quietly.

'What?'

'It's a quote,' she said, turning to look at Beverly.

'What?'

'From a bloke called Egghard Toll. He talks to me on the iPod.'

'Egghead who? Sounds like rubbish to me. The sooner you get rid of that thing the better. You've been acting weird lately, Sadie Smith, and I think you need to pull your head in.'

Sadie looked down to her flat navy 'back-saver' shoes and the dark hairs on her legs that were smothered like a lodged hay paddock against her skin by her beige support hose. Perhaps Bev was right. She had been feeling a little odd lately. One minute she felt incredibly depressed, and the next she found joy and beauty in the oddest things.

This morning, for instance, when she had gone to feed the pigs, she'd gleefully flung the entire crop of Bryan's broad beans into their trough. As the pigs gobbled up their cows' milk and beans, she'd noticed for the very first time their intelligent eyes and the way they looked at her adoringly, all because she was the provider of their food each morning.

She realised the pigs were trying to show her gratitude, and even love, despite the fact that every year she and Bryan had taken the sows' babies away to kill or sell. She had sat with the sows for a time and run her fingertips over their rolling necks, giving them scratches on their thick bristly skin.

With each milking, too, Mavis the cow was less sour in her

demeanour and the poddy calf seemed calmer. Sadie had also taken to scratching the cow and calf, admiring the miracle of their markings, the way the black patches met so perfectly with the white. She saw for the first time how amazing the creatures were. And how obliging. The sudden connection she felt with them had brought tears of happiness to her eyes.

Now in the ute she glanced over to Beverly. Should she mention these strange thoughts? Should she tell her how she'd put the iPod earphones into Mavis's ears and played 'The Prosperity Meditation' while she milked? Mavis had given more milk that morning than ever before.

Sadie looked at Beverly in her town hairdo of home-curled culvert pipes of grey, cemented with hairspray. She noticed how Bev's thick black eyebrows knitted together sternly and her lined mouth was permanently turned down. Perhaps Bev would not be impressed by her putting someone else's iPod in the grimy, waxy ears of a cow. No, best not to mention anything. And yes, thought Sadie, it was best that the iPod went back.

'Can't do a thing,' the dumpy woman at the post office said. 'There's no return address. And it's your name on the label.'

'It isn't. I mean, yes, it's for an S Smith, but that could mean Sue or Steve or Stanley or Sid . . . or . . . or Cyril.'

The woman shrugged. 'I can't take it back. You'll have to keep it. And while you're here, there's another parcel out the back arrived for you yesterday.'

Sadie frowned. 'But I haven't ordered anything.'

The postal worker rolled her eyes and disappeared into the side room. She came back with a box, the same brown packaging with the label on it: *S Smith, Forestdale Road, Edenville, Tasmania.*

'That's not for me.'

'Must be for you.'

'But who's it from?'

Another shrug. 'No return address.'

———❖———

Out in the street, a savage blustery wind blew rain sideways under the post office awning. Sadie drew her coat tight about her and clutched both parcels. Should she open the new one while she waited for Bev? Within seconds curiosity got the better of her, so she set the first parcel down and tore off the tape on the second box. As she did, the packaging fluttered out. Amidst the shredded paper flew hundreds of tiny red paper hearts that swirled down the street. Sadie laughed at the sight. She pulled out a small square mirror with a simple wooden frame. An envelope was tied to it with a golden ribbon, and inside was an embossed card. She read the words out loud.

'Remember, you are loved.'

Sadie looked into the mirror and her big brown eyes stared back at her. They were the eyes of a child. Blinking back tears, she wondered who had sent the mirror. And who loved her? She flipped the card over.

'Remember, you must love your*self*.' Sadie clutched the mirror and note to her chest and shut her eyes.

'Sadie!' Beverly called as she came marching along the street, bags of groceries in each hand, battling the wind. 'I thought you were taking that thing back, not getting more parcels.'

'They wouldn't take it back,' she said, hastily shoving the mirror and note back into the box. 'There's no return address, no company to contact other than the iPod folk and they don't know nothing about it. Post office lady reckons it's someone's internet shopping that's buggered up. So I guess all there's left to do is keep it and enjoy it.'

Bev simply huffed as she hauled her shopping onto the back of the ute, grappled for her keys, then unlocked the cab.

'Let's get going. It's awful bitter today.'

'I don't know if it's bitter, Bev,' said Sadie, loading the parcels onto the floor of the ute. 'We could choose to enjoy this crazy wind and rain, instead of complaining about it. Doesn't it make you want to do something wild?'

'Wild? Like what?'

'Like jump in a puddle? Or . . .' Sadie glanced across the

street to a shopfront newly painted with the words *Wild Child Western Wear*. 'Or go into one of them shops we've never been to. Like that one!' Sadie pointed.

'Are you bonkers? That shop's for young girls. And it'll be full price. You're best off at the op shop. Remember, you're a widow now with no one to provide for you.' Sadie hovered at the tray of Beverly's ute, the wind tossing her frock about, making the daisy pattern dance.

'How old are you, Bev?'

'You know that, Sadie. You baked the cake for my sixtieth just this year.'

'Well, I'm only forty-two. I deserve to go into that new shop. And I deserve to *buy* something. You can wait here or come with me. Your choice.'

Then Sadie Smith crossed the street without looking back.

———◆———

On the drive home, with the bags of new Country Belle clothes and two new pairs of Cuban-heeled western slide shoes sitting on her lap, Sadie looked over to a very silent Beverly and began to laugh.

'Oh, Bev. You look like you've sucked on a lemon – and had another ten shoved up your backside.'

'Excuse me! You've made me late for getting Norris's lunch – and Bryan would be horrified to see you spend money like that.'

'I'm practising abundance. And besides, Norris can get his own lunch. He's thirty, for God's sake! And he has a wife now.'

'Practising what?' Beverly shook her head so her grey curls, dampened now from the rain, wobbled. 'Norris has been working hard on the farm since his father died and he deserves to be looked after. You wouldn't understand.'

'No, I wouldn't, because I've never been a mother, have I, Bev? As you keep reminding me. But on my iPod, Egghard Toll says that some parents can't let go of being a parent, even when their child has grown to be an adult. Poor Norris can't grow up while you do what you do. Bryan's mother was just the same. She smothered Bryan till the day she died.'

Beverly's mouth flapped like a trout.

'Don't you speak ill of Shirley! And what's between me and Norris is my business.' Her eyes narrowed to slits. 'I don't know what's got into you, Sadie, but I don't like it.'

Before Sadie could answer they rounded the mountain bend and spotted a furry lump on the road.

'Road kill! A possum,' Sadie said. Beverly rolled her eyes and pulled over. 'Do you mind if I take it this time, Bev? It'll save me having to shoot something for the dogs tonight. You can have the next one we see. I'm sure there was a roo near the quarry gate that would do for your dogs. Hopefully no one else has taken it.'

Bev sighed. 'You have the bloody possum. Just put it on the bonnet. I don't want it in the tray with my groceries.'

Out on the road, in the blustery cold, Sadie picked up the wet possum by its bushy tail and laid it on the ute at the base of the windscreen.

'Waste not, want not,' she said cheerfully as she got back in, smiling at Beverly, who only shoved the gear stick into first and ground her dentures in frustration as she drove on.

As Sadie stared through the windscreen over the body of the possum, she recalled Muppet Man saying something about 'surrounding yourself with positive people who support you'. She thought of all the times Beverly had berated her, belittled her, silenced her, just as Bryan had done. A small voice in her head became louder and clearer. It told her she deserved better.

'If you don't mind, Bev,' Sadie said, as they neared the turn-off to Edenville, 'you can just drop me at the corner. I'd like to walk the road home, alone.'

'*Walk?* You? You'll chafe your inner thighs again. Remember that time you and Bryan broke down and he sent you to get help? I had to lend you my 3B cream for the rash.'

'*Just stop!*'

As Sadie got out onto the wintry gravel road, Beverly cast her a stinging look. 'Lucky you're not wearing those new fancy new shoes with the heels. You'd break a leg and we'd have to put you down.'

'Oh, I think you've already done that enough, Bev,' Sadie said, as she slammed the ute door and grabbed the possum from the bonnet. She lifted it to wave Bev away, then pulled the iPod earphones from her handbag and shoved them in her ears. Muttering, she clicked on 'The Serenity Journey', gathered up her shopping bags in one hand and her relatively fresh roadkill in the other, and walked on.

As she listened to the music and birdsong meditation, she took in the brightness of the winter sunshine and the way the grasses shone wet from the scudding showers that had earlier blasted their way across the mountainside. At the turn of the road she saw the vista of the valley below and stopped to draw in a deep breath.

'Eden,' she said in amazement. She had grown up here, but it was as if she had never truly seen it before. Today she saw the way the paddocks rolled greenly to the fringes of deep rugged bushland, saw how the creeks carved silver veins through the landscape. Far off in the distance she could hear Michael barking from his chain by the porch, as if guiding her home.

She set out down the hill, feeling uncomfortable at having to walk past the racing stables owned by the rich townies. She and Bryan had nothing to do with them, even though they were neighbours. They had bought the land for a huge price some forty years before and had proceeded to put up white fences and stock the place with sleek horses. Bryan still saw them as intruders and outsiders. He always instructed Sadie to avert her eyes when driving past in summer, because the girls and young men who worked the horses barely wore any clothes on their cinnamon-tanned bodies. On beautiful sunny days,

Sadie sometimes peeked at the girls in bikini tops out feeding the horses, and the men who sometimes rode shirtless with just their chest protectors on, looking like gladiators.

No one was about today, save for some curious horses in their paddock by the road that trotted over to say hello. Sadie savoured the beauty of their shining dark eyes and healthy coats. She had never noticed just how heavenly horses were and she stood looking at them for a time, taking in their very essence.

With the iPod still playing, Sadie didn't hear the clip-clopping on the road until a man on a horse was almost beside her. She looked up, startled, and was instantly struck by his handsomeness. Like his horse, the young man was incredibly fit and beautiful. Lean yet muscular with chiselled features, he cast her a dazzling smile.

'Did you run over that?'

'What?' said Sadie, pulling out the earphones.

Still holding the reins of the jittery thoroughbred, he inclined his helmet-covered head towards the possum. 'Did you run over that? You must be a fast runner.'

Sadie laughed. 'It's for my dogs.'

'Lucky dogs. I'm Michael, by the way,' he said, steadying the horse as it danced on silver-shod hooves.

'Same name as my dog,' she laughed.

'Is he a naughty boy like me?' Michael's eyes twinkled.

'You don't look like a naughty boy,' Sadie said. If she'd

had a son, she would've wanted him to look like this boy. His blue eyes were kind, and crinkled at the corners, and his skin glowed from outdoor activity.

'You live on the place next door, don't you?' he asked.

'Yes.'

'And your dad died a little while back, didn't he?'

'Not my dad, my husband.' It wasn't the first time she'd been mistaken for Bryan's daughter.

'Oh? I see. I'm sorry.' Michael considered her again. 'So, what's your name?'

'Sadie.'

'Sadie? As in Sadie the cleaning lady?'

'Yes.'

'So, are you offering?' Sadie looked puzzled. 'Offering to clean, I mean.'

Sadie set down her possum, her parcels and her shopping and thought for a moment. On impulse she heard herself saying, 'Well, I could be after a job. Do you have one?'

'Leave it with me, Sadie the cleaning lady. I'll ask the boss. We sure could do with some help.'

At this point, the highly strung filly lost her patience and, instead of merely fidgeting with the bit in her mouth, began to paw the ground and swing about.

'Settle, petal!' Michael said to the horse, before squeezing her on, then calling back over his shoulder, 'Gotta go! But come back tomorrow, Sadie, my sweet.'

Sadie, my sweet? Sadie felt blood rush to her cheeks. What a lovely young man. His mother would be so proud of him.

'Don't forget to take your possum,' she heard him call again.

Thoughtful too, she decided happily, as she began to walk the last few kilometres home.

At the woodshed, Sadie set the possum on the block and raised the axe. The little claws fell away easily with her expert chop. She bent to retrieve them, throwing them into the forty-four-gallon drum so the dogs couldn't eat them. As she picked up the knife, she noticed the possum's soft fur of mottled grey, black and brown and thought how beautiful it was. She had never thought of a possum as beautiful before and surprised herself by hearing the voice in her head blessing the life of the possum.

Flipping the stiff carcass on its back, Sadie was about to slice it up the middle to gut it when she noticed a tiny tail sticking out from a pouch. She frowned. When she pulled on the tail, out came a baby possum that was so small she could cup it in one hand. It had huge brown eyes and a pretty little pink nose. It was just starting to grow fur. Sadie could feel the feebleness of its life and its little feather breaths on her palm.

Before she knew it she found herself slumped down on the

wet cold grass, her head bowed, the baby cradled in her hands as if she were taking communion. She stared at the possum and, as she did, she felt the last gasp of life leave its body and saw the light fade from its eyes. As she clutched the baby possum to her breast, she heard herself moan with anguish, a deep, pain-drenched cry. It set the dogs howling.

She scrunched her eyes shut, and the memory of the humiliation of Bryan's rough grope at her crotch with his cruel hands came flooding back.

'C'mon, show me your fanny, woman,' she heard him say. She remembered the way he had shoved into her in the middle of the night like a boar, then rolled off her and snored back to sleep. She recalled how the terrible stomach cramps had begun on the eve of her twenty-first birthday. Then, in the night, she'd gone to the toilet and a dark bloody thing had slithered out from between her legs onto the bathroom floor. The baby had looked more possum than human.

Bryan hadn't taken her to the doctor. He'd simply torn up old bed sheets for her to jam between her legs. The next morning, she'd watched from the bedroom window as he'd taken the baby in a chaff sack and buried it beneath a cold moaning pine in the front paddock. For weeks after, Sadie dreamt of the pigs digging up the sack and gobbling the baby down. Then she'd wake up crying, hating the pigs. Hating Bryan. Hating life.

'Turning on the tears to get attention, are ya?' Bryan had

said to her, a week after it happened. 'For Christ's sake, give it a rest, you stupid woman.'

From that day on, Sadie Smith's heart shut down and she had never cried again.

But here she was now, out by the woodshed, awash with grief. Crying for the baby beneath the pine and her other children never born. For the wasted years when she was closed off, unconscious to the beauty around her and the power within her.

Sadie cried and kept on crying until the cockatoos began to roost for the night, high above her in the big old gum tree. When at last she was stiff with cold, Michael came to her and licked her face. She smiled at the little dog and hauled herself up.

With a shovel, in the dark, she trudged to the pine tree and buried the possum and its baby near where her child lay. Then she went inside and stoked the fire. Michael settled down on the fireside mat as Sadie put on her iPod, shut her eyes and let the sound of rain wash clean through her.

———————◆———————

The summer heat at the stables was so intense that black spiders fell dead from the tin roof onto the concrete, prompting Sadie's workmate, Tania, to scream from time to time as she mucked out the stables. The other stable staff worked through

their jobs listlessly and sprayed themselves more than the race-
horses in the wash bay. At lunchtime they took to the shade of
a twisted willow on the lawn beside the smoko room. There
they lolled like overheated lionesses. Sadie lounged with them,
while Michael the dog panted by her side.

Sadie's hair, longer now, was tied up in a mass of thick
rich brown curls, and her legs, no longer hidden under long
baggy clothes, were honey-tanned and smooth from Tania's
recent waxing. For the past eight months, with encourage-
ment from the girls, Sadie had walked to and from work,
and she could now fit into her new size 14 Wild Child shorts.
She tugged them down over her Rembrandt thighs as she
stood up.

'Where are you going?' mumbled Sally from where she lay
on the grass in her red bikini top.

'The saddle blankets.' Sadie pointed to the stiff squares on
the fence railing. 'They're dry. Cooked even.'

'Sadie,' groaned Sally. 'Stop working! Just relax. It's too
hot to do anything.'

'But I'm not done for the day,' she said.

'Yes, you are,' Steph said. 'You're a workaholic. You put
us all to shame!'

Sadie sat back down. Sally and Steph were right. Today
was not the day to do much of anything.

'And for God's sake, Sadie, take that shirt off. You make me
feel even hotter just looking at you,' came Tania's sleepy voice

as she rolled over, revealing her own tanned torso beneath her skimpy singlet.

'But . . .'

'Off!'

Reluctantly Sadie pulled off her shapeless man's work shirt. Underneath, she wore a new Western Wear black singlet that read, in hot pink, 'In your Buckin' Dreams'. Steph wolf-whistled.

'Michael's going to faint when he sees your knockers out on display. They are something to behold.'

'Cripes,' Sally said. 'You should get 'em out more often, Sadie. I would if I had 'em. Not like these two little pimples.'

Sadie looked down at herself and giggled. With no Bryan to demand chops for breakfast, roast for lunch and casseroles and dessert for dinner, Sadie had rediscovered her waist and beneath the fat she found a body already nicely toned from farm work. She resisted the self-conscious urge to put her top back on when she heard a diesel engine announcing Michael's return from his beer run to town. Beauty comes from within, she told herself as she hoisted up her bra strap.

They all cheered as Michael came around the corner with bags of groceries, an esky and a box perched precariously on top of it.

'Snags, beer, munchies! It's party time!' He waved the box at Sadie. 'This was at the post office for you.'

Sadie sat up, frowning.

'But I didn't order nothing.'

There had been no more mystery parcels since the iPod and mirror had arrived months before. Every day Sadie was grateful for the original mistake. Every day, she did her morning affirmations in the mirror and her milking meditation with Mavis. The iPod now also held a special 'Sadie mix' of new music downloaded for her by the girls. Music even sexier than Tom Jones.

She'd thought the days of surprise packages were over. But here was another one with no return address and the very same label.

'Go on. Open it!' Tania urged.

Sadie tore off the brown packaging to reveal a box featuring a picture of a buffed half-naked cowboy with washboard stomach.

Michael, Steph, Sally and Tania whooped and laughed.

Puzzled, Sadie looked from them to the box. 'What is it?'

'What is it?' Steph said, and the rest of them fell about laughing. 'Oh, come on. You ordered it!'

'No, I didn't. But what is it?'

'Oh, geez, Sadie, what planet are you from?' said Michael. 'It's a blow-up doll! You know . . . a jiggy-jig doll.'

'A what? What's it for?'

That set them off on another round of spluttering hysterics. Eventually, Michael wiped away his tears, and looked sympathetically at Sadie.

'Give him to me.'

Words failed Sadie as Michael dragged out what looked like a deflated mannequin wearing cowboy chaps and not much else. He began to blow it up, while Sally read out the print on the side of the box.

'*Hold on, cowgirls, 'cause here's a cowboy that's good to ride. Enjoy hours of galloping pleasure from this lifelike inflatable adult toy, with attachments. Batteries not included.*'

'Batteries! Quick! I'll get some batteries!' Steph said, leaping up and dashing inside the smoko room.

'She's not going to use him now, Steph!' called Tania. 'At least I hope you're not, Sadie.'

'I don't know . . .'

'It says lifelike,' Sally said, holding the inflated doll up next to Michael and frowning. 'I suppose he looks more real than you,' she teased.

'You'll never know,' Michael teased back.

'But what's it *for*?' Sadie asked again.

'You seriously don't know?' Sally said. 'Oh, Sadie, you poor darling.'

'Wait, we haven't got out the attachments,' Michael said with a grin. 'Then the penny should drop for our sweet Sadie.'

―――――◆―――――

Tipsy on beer and high on life, Sadie dragged Eddie out of the water and threw him on his back. His inflated, digitless limbs pointed to the early evening sky.

'The stars, eh, Eddie, my love! You want me to look at the stars? Oh, you're a romantic bugger,' Sadie said, laughing as she stared into the doll's vacant eyes. She turned to see the giant yellow disc of a full moon rising up over the mountain and casting golden ripples on the dam's dark surface.

To the west, the sun had sunk behind the mountain range so that the sky there also shone gold, punctuated by a bright evening star. Sadie felt the day's heat still radiating from the soil beneath her bare feet, and the droplets of dam water on her skin made her whole body tingle. She sucked in a breath. It felt so good to be alive at this very moment. She reached out to hold Eddie's squashy stump of a hand.

'Oh, Eddie,' she sighed. She rolled over onto her stomach and eyed the picnic blanket that was scattered with the remains of their summer feast. There was a ravaged platter of strawberries, raspberries, cherries and blackberries, all gathered from her garden, and the remains of their feast of home-cooked chook, crisp snowpeas, and freshly baked bread rolls smeared with handmade butter. She picked up a strawberry and offered it to Eddie.

'Not hungry?' Sadie popped the ripe fruit in her mouth, the sweet juices exploding on her tongue. 'More for me.'

'Hey, you two!' Michael shouted from the dam. 'Come back in!'

Sadie smiled as she watched Steph with Sally on her

shoulders. With a powerful leap, Steph tossed Sally up high so she speared the air with flailing limbs and shrieks before hitting the water, sending up a fountain of spray. Screams, laughter and shouts rang out across the water. Michael called to Sadie again.

'Give me back Eddie! I need him to float on so I can drink my beer!'

Sadie watched as Michael came out of the water, wearing only his shorts. His tanned torso gleamed wet in the moonlight.

'C'mon, Sadie,' he said. 'We want Eddie.'

'But *I* want him.'

Michael dropped down next to her, his broad smooth chest rising and falling with each breath.

'I'll get jealous,' he teased.

'But a handsome young blow-up boy is just what's been missing from my life,' Sadie joked.

'Is it now?' Michael said, his voice deeper and more serious. 'Do you actually know how to use him?'

'Ah, well, no, not really. But I'm sure he'll have instructions.'

'Why bother, when you can have the real thing?' Sadie jumped with pleasant surprise as Michael's hand gently brushed her thigh. He leant towards her. 'Perhaps later, I could help you with the instructions. But really, why use him when you could find out how a real cowboy rides? Sadie, I'm offering.'

Sadie bit her lip. 'Why would you do that?'

'Because I like you . . . and it would be fun.'

Sadie glanced at his beautiful young face. He was looking earnestly at her. A million questions raced in her head.
Was he really being serious or simply teasing her? A hundred
doubts, a hundred fears rushed in at her. The old Sadie began
ranting at her about her ugliness, her fatness, her uselessness,
the sin of it.

But there in the moonlight with her new friends around her,
she managed to silence the voice that tried to drag her down.
Be in the moment, she heard the calm voice of the new Sadie
say. *Live life to the full. Live for now. And don't let your fears
stop you. Life is not meant to be so serious.*

'Well? Would you like?' Michael asked.

She leant towards him, close enough so that she could smell
him. She brushed her lips on his shoulder and could almost
taste the dam water on his smooth skin. Then she looked up
at him with her big brown eyes.

'I would like. Very much.'

'Good. I'll meet you for lessons later, but, first, playtime
with the girls. Then I'll be back to claim my cougar!'

'Your what?'

'Oh, never mind, Sadie,' he laughed , 'just be prepared for
the time of your life!'

Michael leapt up, tucking Eddie under his arm like a bat-
tering ram, and sprinted towards the water with a battle cry
that caused the girls to scream with mirth.

Sadie lay back in the paddock, looked up at the moon and

smiled. Tonight, the mystery of the parcels had finally been solved. It was simply the synchronicity of the universe, she decided. The parcels had been heaven-sent.

———◆———

Across the Indian Ocean, as the sun was slowly bringing a beautiful dawn light to the African hills, Sally Smith of Forest-dale Road, Edenville, Tanzania, rolled her rather hippo-like body over in bed. She wondered sadly how it was possible that the Tanzanian postal system had failed her a third time! She swallowed down a bitter taste and vowed never to go internet shopping after drinking too many gins again.

McCubbin's Lost Child

She was lost. The young girl wiped away the stream of tears with the back of her hand, leaving a smear of dampened dust across her sweating face. She clung to the corner of her pinafore and took in another shuddering breath so her sobs could begin again. The deafening sound of cicadas shrilled in her ears. Their chorus of screams from tiny papery wings made her dizzy. An ant climbed the ladder of laces on her boots and with flickering antennae inspected her thick black woollen stockings.

The girl wanted to sit under a tree, but there seemed to be no shade. The sun dappled through thin drooping gum leaves and spread onto the crackling dry yellow grass. In the distance, the grass misted white in the haze of heat. Soil baked in the sun, so that its warmth rose beneath her, making her skin prickle with sweat under her long blue dress. Her heavy, thickly braided hair clung to her neck and her straw hat made tiny impressions on her forehead that itched and itched. Lost.

'Oh, why couldn't I have been a Toulouse-Lautrec girl?' she screamed into the vacancy of the dense bush that surrounded her lonely form. The artist had layered the paint on so thickly in gum-leaf blues and greens that she could not, no matter how hard she strained, see her way to the frame surrounding the painting.

'Ohhh!' she sobbed.'Why me? Why *me*? Stuck in a Fredrick McCubbin! In a dull blue dress and pinafore!'

No one had a hope of seeing her pretty face, so shaded by the brim of her straw hat and covered with her hand. Viewers of the artwork had to peer through saplings to see her slim and solitary figure. They immediately felt pity and even sorrow for the girl, who was so hopelessly lost.

'Arrrghh!' She kicked at the dry grass under her feet in frustration. Oh, to be a Toulouse-Lautrec girl, seducing the eyes of the viewer with the flash of a long stockinged leg from beneath a billowing white petticoat. The pink, inviting flesh of a thigh peeping from a garter belt. Red lips, long black gloves and full flashing skirts. Perhaps even a glimpse of full white bosom. The young girl looked down at her pinafore that bore no shape of a full white bosom at all. Fredrick McCubbin had laid the oil on so thickly all she could see were solid folds of material. He hadn't given her a chance. Contained here, in this blur of bush. Lost. Tiny glimpses of sky were all she had.

There wasn't even a waft of campfire smoke just to give her the smallest clue.

A man with spectacles and grey shoes softly trod the floor of the National Gallery of Victoria and peered at the painting. His hands cupped together behind his back.

'Even an Andy Warhol would've been better than this!' she screamed at the man. 'Having bright-orange hair and cherry-red lips and being surrounded by tomato soup cans would be a better option!'

But the man didn't hear her. He only felt sorrow for the lost girl in the bush. Black cockatoos mimicked her screeches as they shimmered through the treetops. The sun carried in the gloss of their wings. The man shuffled away over the linoleum floor in the empty gallery.

'Damn you! Damn you, Fredrick McCubbin!' Her sobs rose again. 'Oh, and to be hung in this gallery!' Tears flowed and mixed with sweat on her face. Why couldn't it have been somewhere with more class and flamboyance? Not to mention more art-lovers. Why not the Osterreichische Galerie Belvedere? She could have been the beautiful girl in Gustav Klimt's *The Kiss*.

'Ah . . . *Der Kuss*,' she sighed. Such a clear view of beauty. A face with rosy pink cheeks flushed by the touch of her slim-fingered lover. His dark hands on her soft white skin. Eyes shut in lovers' bliss. And all shimmering in gold cloth. Her head tipped back in a swoon as his dark skin and wanting lips place the kiss on her cheek. Flowers entwined in rich red hair. Making love in soft green meadows filled with spring blooms of purples, cornflower blues and pinks.

'Damn, damn, damn!' cried the young girl as a blowfly buzzed around her head, landed on her cheek and crawled across her skin. She looked at the grey trunks of the gum trees and the dull greens of the wattle. Dried brown bark peeled its way down the trunk of a tree.

'No lover would ever want to lay me down in this,' she said to no one in her lonely lost world. Amidst the dry grass were little ant hills that teemed with the busyness of ants. 'Especially here. And especially not in this dress!'

The girl began sobbing softly again and looking hard through the trees for the gilded edge of the frame. But there. Yes, there! She felt it. In her lost world she felt it. Just a glimmer of gratitude. The slightest flicker of gladness in her heart. *At least she didn't look like daggy old Mona Lisa!*

Mother Nature

Wild wings fluttered against the grimy glass.

'There's a bird stuck in the wood heater again,' Valerie called wearily to nobody listening. She took the old towel in her hands. Her parents had brought it back from Hawaii for her when she was a child, and it had been her prize possession. She had loved the image of a girl dancing the hula under a palm tree. Now faded and scratchy, it had become the household bird-catching towel, and lay ready in the wood basket beside the sleeping heater.

'We must put some netting over that chimney to stop them getting in,' she said, again to nobody. A terrified beady bird's eye watched as Valerie opened the door of the heater. The hula girl's outstretched arms danced nearer and nearer into the dark corners of the firebox. A flurry of wings whipped up storms of fine ash from last winter's fires. Valerie no longer muttered useless words of consolation to the birds. The daily ritual had made her bitter towards the greasy-looking starlings.

'We really should knock them on the head so they don't keep coming back,' she said, wincing as she clasped the towel tightly around the bird's bony body. 'After all, they are introduced,' she called over her shoulder to her husband and children, who didn't reply. The term 'introduced' always amused her. She smiled vaguely as she imagined a British soldier walking down the gangplank of a tall ship with a pair of starlings on his arm, their yellow-grey claws clasping his stiff woollen uniform. The soldier formally introduces the birds to the vast continent: 'Mr and Mrs Starling, I'd like to introduce you to Madame Terra Australis,' with a slight bow. The large lady continent would not be at all amused at receiving such unattractive and demanding guests, thought Valerie. She had mentioned the annoying starlings to her brother on the phone when she first moved into the house.

'You should put chicken wire around the front of the heater and you'd have an instant aviary and a great talking point in your home,' her brother had joked. He didn't understand. In his tidy city house with his tidy city wife, all he ever did was get into his freshly dust-busted car and drive over bitumen to his tidy city office. Once, on a visit to her brother's house, Valerie had delighted in offering half a biscuit to the black beak of a semi-tame magpie. It wavered and warbled on her sister-in-law's Hills Hoist. Her sister-in-law had warned, 'If that bird shits all over my washing, I'll know who to blame,' and the bird was banished to the corrugated-iron rooftops.

Valerie stood at her back door with the starling wrapped in the towel. It would be so easy to kill it. Just pick up a brick and drop it on its little head. But Valerie opened the towel and the bird flew chirruping and terrified into a cloudy sky. It settled on the machinery shed where it perched on steel, puffing beneath drab feathers.

<hr />

Around springtime in the old house baby birds screamed and shrilled to be fed above Valerie's head while she tried to write her shopping list. Scaled claws scratched above in the old wooden ceilings, and dust and bits of grassy flotsam dropped onto the freshly wiped kitchen table. Should she get a cat and put it in the roof? Should she poison them? But she knew she couldn't kill anything. Some mornings she just couldn't face picking up the bird towel and rescuing another introduced species as hideous as the starling.

'I'm leaving it for someone else to do,' she'd call. But each time the front door slammed shut with another departure for the day and the house grew quiet she would hear the scratching of claws on glass and feel a stab of guilt for being so cruel. Sighing, angry, she'd pick up the towel.

After holidays she dreaded coming back to the house. Birds

had scratched, shat, panicked and fluttered until they died in piles in the dark ashy prison of the heater. Then the flies came into the chimney until the hollow carcasses of birds writhed with tiny maggots. The smell of death permeated every room of the little farmhouse – she even smelt dead birds on her pillow. But no one else seemed to care.

'Right. I'll bloody well do it myself,' Valerie spat, after a bird had escaped from the hula-dancing girl and flown headlong, *splat*, into a window. It sat on the carpet dazed and shitting. Valerie stomped off to the shed to find some chicken wire and a ladder. Rummaging around in the shed, she heard the annoyed question from her husband, 'What are you doing there, woman?'

'I'm going to block those birds once and for all,' she told him, but her husband didn't hear. In his hand was a letter.

'There's a job going – driving tractors on a station in Queensland. Hundred bucks a day, the house and the rest thrown in, starting in two weeks,' said the large silhouette in the shed doorway.

'I guess there's no need to fix the chimney then,' she said tiredly.

She wrapped their life in newspaper and put it into boxes and stretched screeching brown tape tight over the top. On departure day, he slammed down the bonnet of the car. 'Right to go!' he said, and the lot of them crammed in, kids, dogs, eskys, their life. Looking up at the chimney she said to herself,

'Goodbye, birds!' and sat back and smiled at the sound of tyres crunching over the gravel drive for the last time.

In the new house air-conditioning hummed and cupboards opened up wide with promise. Valerie smiled. There was no wood heater. No cracks in the ceiling. In the bathroom she stroked fingertips over the new easy-to-clean sink.

'I now declare this toilet open,' she said as she lifted the toilet lid. Suddenly she jumped and let out a shriek. There, greener than any manmade plastic, was a big shiny frog staring up at her with glassy black eyes. Its toes were suctioned fast to the bowl. In a flash, she flushed. A mass of frogs cascaded and tumbled out from under the rim. Frogs' legs, brown and speckled. Green and cream. Suckers desperately trying to avoid being swept away by the rapids into the S-bend pipe.

'Damn,' she muttered. She'd have to find a tree or go behind a shed. There was no way she could pee on a frog. That evening, as they sat on the newly positioned couch watching the newly placed TV, she let out a yip as a frog hopped across the carpet and plopped itself under her couch. At the sink, Valerie sucked in a shock of air as a green frog dashed its way upside down across the gauze on the window to snap hungrily at a moth. In the shower she yelped as a little brown frog leapt when she moved her bottle of New Lady skin polisher. It hopped up the tiled wall, thinking it was perfectly hidden under the soap dish. But she could still see one of its little circular toes. Dripping wet, she rummaged around in an unpacked box to find her bird towel. She sighed sadly. Her bird towel had now become a frog towel.

The dogs were barking at the new strange night sounds. Valerie got up to silence them, floundering in the dark to find the switch. With horror her toes squelched on something soft. She stifled a scream. When she flicked on the light she saw a grey gecko scurrying across the floor and up the wall to hide behind the newly hung clock. It left a little black speck of poo as it ran. It stuck to the wall like adhesive mouse dirt.

'The frog towel will have to double as a gecko towel,' she sighed. As she lay beneath the whirring ceiling fan, enveloped in Queensland heat, she told herself to give it time. She'd get used to it. After all, frogs and geckos weren't introduced and if she tried really hard, she would probably get to like them. In the morning she crossed a spongy buffalo-grass lawn to introduce herself to the stockman's wife next door and ask her what to do about the frogs and geckos.

'I used to think they were cute,' she said to the leather-lined woman drawing up the smoke of a Winfield Blue, 'but sharing a house with them annoys the crap out of me.'

'Dirty little buggers,' the woman said as she exhaled smoke. The stockman's wife couldn't kill the frogs, but was unwilling to let her captives free outside, for fear they would invade her territory again. 'Freezer,' she said, drawing another puff, 'I stick 'em in the freezer. That way, the freezer's killin' 'em, not me. At one stage I had ninety frogs in there, eh!'

She wheezed as she laughed. Valerie tried hard to hide the horror on her face as she thanked the stockman's wife and said she'd better get back to her washing. When she was nearly across the lawn, the stockman's wife yelled out, 'It's the mice and the cane toads you gotta watch!' Valerie smiled and waved before shutting herself inside the house.

When she saw her first cane toad she was overcome with loathing. It was so ugly it was almost painful to look at.

'How could anyone have introduced them to this country?' she said to her children, who were busy poking the toad with a stick. She wasn't sure if it was the cane toad at her back doorstep or the little torpedo-shaped mice poo she found in her bed, her cupboards and on her kitchen bench that made her hiss, 'It's war.' She pulled on her pink washing-up gloves and spooned bright-green poison pellets into little cupcake papers.

'Dinner's served,' she said between clenched teeth as she put the poison in the corners of the house. On the porch she pitched deadly capfuls of Dettol onto the backs of the toads and with a hideous mix of delight and horror watched them hop off to die in the leafy garden. As her husband slept she smiled with steely satisfaction as she heard the mice rustle poison pellets behind her bedside table.

But soon Valerie was no longer satisfied with poisoning. She wanted more. She wanted bodies. A massacre. So she could line them up, count and gloat. From the local store she bought little wooden traps. She tried different types of bait in each one.

Beef gristle, cooked rice, baked beans, even sultanas. From her bed she heard traps snap shut. The temptation to jump up to look at her victims was too much. If she was quick enough, she'd get to see them twitching in the traps before they died.

As the body count grew so did Valerie's passion. Counting them was the best. She loved to pick the mice up by the tail and lay them in rows on newspaper before throwing them in the big wheelie bin outside. On the back of her shopping list, Valerie drew a neat little table and kept score of her killings each week. She hid it from her husband and children in a recipe book. She felt delighted by it, like a serial killer would, she supposed. But the mice were not enough for Valerie.

One warm night, when a fine misty rain was falling, Valerie's family awoke to hear her shrieking on the lawn outside. Scrambling out of bed they met in the hall, confused and dazed. Valerie's husband flung open the back door and switched on the light. There was Valerie, barefoot in her floral nightdress on the lawn, wearing a head torch. She was looking down at a cane toad, which was sitting immobilised in the beam of torchlight. She had in her hands her eldest boy's three-iron golf club, which gleamed like a sword.

'Fore!' she shouted into the night and the club struck the cane toad with a dull *thwhack*. She let out a shriek of delight as the cane toad flew a few metres and then landed twitching with what looked like pink brains oozing from its eyes.

'What the hell are you doing, woman?' the husband hissed.

'Have you gone mad? You'll wake up the whole bloomin' station!'

'But they're introduced, darling!' Valerie chirped in delight, and her crazy eyes searched the beam of light to find the next toad. 'Fore!' she cried again and swung the club high into the night air.

The Wife

She thought it would change after she married him. Her hands in the hot water seemed to make her blood boil and her face burn. He had been late again and Jenny was sure she could smell the sex of another woman in his hair. Over a greasy baking dish she watched him through the grimy kitchen window. He was sharpening a knife on a stone. Her thoughts simmered in her head in the hot little kitchen. She wiped her numb red hands on a tea towel and pushed open the sagging screen door.

Call to him from the verandah like a good little wife . . .

'What are you up to?' He was just off to the yard. A couple of ewes had gone down with pregnancy toxemia and had to have their throats cut. 'Can I come with you?' He turned his back.

'I'll just grab a coat.' *Sweet wifey voice.*

Her hot cheeks cooled in the icy wind as she ran to him.

He was at the dog kennels, smiling, talking softly to his best bitch.

'Hello, my lady.' He stroked the lean red dog with big brown hands. Tender hands running firmly over the dog's ribby sides. The bitch stood on her back legs and rested her front paws on his thighs, her claws digging into the fabric of his jeans near his crotch, her sincere brown eyes gazing into his. Jenny stood watching, hands clenched around old tissues in her pockets.

Touch me like that. Look at me like that. Your good little wife.

He unclipped the chain and Nel bounded away to sniff and squat in the long grass, always with an eye on him, and he with his eyes on her.

'You're not coming on heat, are you, my ol' hussy?' He whistled her, and lifted Nel to inspect her swelling vagina beneath her wagging tail. 'You old tart, Nellie.' He held her soft tan jowls in both hands and looked at her face. Jenny tried to swallow the foulness she seemed to taste.

'You coming?' he said.

Just as Jenny got into the ute, Nel leapt on her lap.

'Get down!' She pushed at the dog. He laughed and told the dog to get in the back. As he drove, Nel leant over the side and smelt the air as it rushed past. The dusty air in the cab annoyed Jenny and she rubbed the paw marks on her jeans over and over until her thighs became hot. On the gravel road to the yards, a car passed them. A small blonde head and a wave of the hand. Nel barked once and wagged her tail as the car sped by.

Was that where you had your cock last night?

She searched for a clue on his face. A muscle flickered beneath the skin of his shaven jaw.

The ewes were both cast. Tossed out of the yards by the men who had crutched them. The grass beneath them was limp and white and they had worn patches away to mud where their hooves had scraped the ground. Hooves galloping nowhere, over and over in pain. Their bellies were swollen with lambs and their breath was short and quick.

'Think of the poor little lambs dying inside,' Jenny said.

'They'd have carked it long ago. Give us a lift,' her husband said.

Jenny took the bony back legs in her hands. The flies buzzed madly around. Blackening blood and fluid like caramel oozed from the ewe. Jenny turned her head away from the stench. He had hold of the front legs and he swung the sheep high and hard. On the ute's tray Nel sniffed and licked at the rear ends of the sheep.

'Get out of it, Nel,' growled Jenny.

'She's right,' he said as he opened the door of the ute. They drove over short winter pasture. Rain had brought the freshest green out of the earth. Spring was coming. Jenny wound down the window and felt the sun on her face and the cold wind. It seemed to rush right through her.

'This'll do.' He switched off the engine and dragged the
ewes off the ute's tray to a fallen tree. Its trunk was grey with
death even though its roots remained in the black living soil.
He grabbed the knife, placed a hand on the ewe's muzzle and
pulled her head back. Her throat was tight. Prodding with
his fingers, he found the hinge of her jaw. Jenny watched and
pulled her coat around her as he put the point of the blade
just below the jaw. He drove it through skin and wool, with a
grunt. Quickly he ripped the knife out so the ewe's legs jerked
rapidly. He brought the knife back into the red of her gaping
neck and drew her head back sharply twisting and severing.
Blood pulsed and spilled onto black earth. The muscle in his
jaw twitched. Jenny watched the life drain from the ewe's
yellow eyes. She looked for the soul rising to heaven but saw
nothing. She leaned close to the body to see if she could feel
the soul rising up through her. But she couldn't feel anything.
It had been like that when her little one had died inside her.
She hadn't felt the soul leave. She looked at the flex of the
muscles in his arms. At the line that made his mouth.

Does it excite you when you kill?

The wind whistled through the ute. He wiped the blade
on the wool of the animal, growing colder in the chilly wind.
Nel lapped at the blood that spilt on the earth. His bloodied
hand stroked her muscular back. The bitch shook in excitement. Jenny slammed the door of the ute and sat hunched in
the front seat as he reached for the second ewe to kill.

Later, back at the house, Jenny watched him from the kitchen window. In the dying light beneath a pepper tree he sat on Nel's log kennel for a long time watching her eat her dog nuts and bones. He gently stroked Nel's ears and talked to her. He lifted her and nuzzled his face into Nel's. Then he walked to the car, started it and drove away. He drove away into town.

Jenny put her hands in the hot water so her blood boiled again. Red skin scalded. She sat for a long time staring at their wedding photo. Her toes froze. It was dark. It was late. The wind rattled the old windows and lifted the corner of the tin roof. It sounded like lovers in a cast-iron bed. It got faster and faster. The lovers. Jenny picked up the knife lying on the sink and ran outside into the madness of the winter wind. No moon, just blackness. Her hair flew about her face. She started the ute, switched on the lights and backed it from the shed. Outside, over the grumble of the engine, she could still hear the lovers in the roof. They were going even faster now. Banging in the cast-iron bed. Thin green fingers of the pepper tree branches scraped and bashed on the ute as she parked it near the kennels. In the headlights she found the gleaming chain which lay in the dust and began to pull it towards her, Nel whimpering and resisting. She located the jaw bone and pressed her finger into the soft spot beneath it and pulled Nel's head back. She placed her knee on the dog's stomach to stop her squirming and tightened her neck. Nel whined.

Plunge the knife in and twist it out. Pull the head back and sever and twist until the neck cracks. Good little wife. Good wifey wife.

Nel's whines became a gurgle from her windpipe. Her paws jerked in the air. Her blood spilt on the earth. Jenny wiped the knife over the dog's gold and brown coat. Then she went back to the house. She filled the kitchen sink and washed the knife in hot, hot water. The lovers in the roof had stopped. The baby in her head had stopped crying. She closed her eyes. Now, perhaps, her husband would see her.

The Way of Things

Wind in the roof wails *woo, wooo, woooo* while a woman wails on the floor of a pink-tiled bathroom. Her cries echo on in the high-ceiling home. '*Oh. Oh. Oh!*' She is curled up and wrapped in cold. Cold porcelain, cold skin, cold bones. A black cloud burdened with stinging rain sweeps over a bare hill. It hits the big stone house and the woman cries out again at the cold. Guttering hits on wood. *Thut, thut, thut.* It reminds her, and her wails rise up again as the wind whooshes in the big empty house. Scudding icy drops smash coldness against the window. The *pit, pit, pit* of the rain turns to a cold grey roar with the hurtle of the wind. The curled woman feels the rain sting on her brain. It hits the pink and grey fire with a sizzle. She hears it. *Phisss, phisss, phisss.* Blue-pink fingers clutch into hair and pull and pull. Above, high on a sandstone wall the wind lifts tin and hits it on stone. *Thwack, thwack, thwack.*

An old screen door dances devilishly with the lusty, gusty wind and shrieks and claps. *Reeeeek . . . bang . . . reeeek . . . bang . . . reeek . . . bang.* Leaves skitter and scatter along edges of walls and then peel themselves free. Tossed away into the air. Branches of old trees bend to the storm and creak and snap.

Someone is whistling somewhere. A high whistle, high in the tree. 'Perhaps it is him,' says a voice in the woman's brain. 'Perhaps it is him whistling to the dogs.' The rope on the branch etches its form into green bark. Back and forth with the wind. *Urrrrck urrrck urrrck.* The dead weight of the man is lifted by the storm so that his body bumps and thuds against the trunk. *Thudud, thudud.* His clothes swish and *flap* against his skin and his hair whips around his cold grey face. Farmer's fingers, curled, drip wet from the rain. The woman hears him whistle and cry out in the storm. The rain has come. But it has come too late. He whooshes and whistles in her ears so she curls up and screams so loudly that she can only hear the storm in her brain. Pink veins pop in the whites of her eyes as she shrivels and swivels on pink tiles. Screaming now in the pink bathroom. She doesn't know why she is in the bathroom. She only knows she chose the colour herself years ago when the sun shone. She only knows the dogs have all been shot on their chains and he is hanging in an old oak in the storm outside the big old house.

The Handy Man

It has been ten years since the neat-as-a-pin newsreader with lacquered hair and painted white teeth read the cue cards declaring the operation a success. Now, in a darkened room smelling of tinned spaghetti and burnt toast, Martin Swain uses his old hand to press rewind and play on the remote control.

The suit-clad newsreader springs onto the screen again. 'Australian businessman Martin Swain, the world's first hand transplant patient, was released from a Los Angeles hospital today with surgeons declaring the forty-hour operation a success . . .'

The present-day Martin, slumped in his stained chair, winces as he watches the footage showing his younger self smiling from his hospital bed with his new hand bandaged tightly in a sling. He looks at the hand that now lies limp on the tatty arm of his chair. The hand plucks at the chair, which oozes foam stuffing onto the threadbare carpet. He examines the hand's hairy knuckles and stubby fingernails, and curses it for the millionth time. He holds up his slim businessman's hand next to the stubby stitched-on hand and in his mind for the umpteenth time replays the scenario . . .

Neither his wife nor his girlfriend objected to the hand to begin with, but the first signs of trouble appeared just days after the operation. Driving home from the doctor's surgery after the bandages were removed, Martin was amazed to find his newly stitched hand flinging itself onto his wife's knee.

'Are you all right, Martin?' she said, trying to concentrate on driving through the afternoon traffic. The fingers, still stained with iodine, travelled under her neatly pleated skirt. Martin's eyes darted from the hand to his wife's face as the out-of-control fingers crawled and kept crawling. With his original hand, Martin quickly reached over and caught his new hand in the nick of time, just before it reached the cotton gusset of her control-brief pantyhose.

'Fine, thank you,' he said, and nervously cleared his throat.

For a few days after that, relations with his wife improved dramatically, breathing fresh life into what had become a stale and routine marriage. Despite some post-operative grogginess and a good deal of soreness in the stitched area, the hand fumbled in Martin's wife's dressing-gown most evenings before bed. And in the dead of night, the hand crawled towards her under the shadowy floral sheets, even as Martin slept.

'Oh! Martin,' yelped his wife in nervous delight.

The hand even made the girlfriend giggle and squirm, and for the first time distracted her from asking when he was going to leave his wife. Martin followed his new hand's every move with virile glee. But at night he was sure he dreamt of its previous owner. In his dreams, a leering, gold-toothed sailor with the tattoo of a buxom mermaid on his upper arm slurred to Martin, 'Come on, sonny, go another one. Take another lass. So warm and fleshy.' The sailor laughed a gravelly laugh as he took Martin by the hand, and in his dreams they sailed from port to port taking whichever whore they pleased with a toss of a bank bill, peeled from a fat wad of notes by the hairy stubby hand. The dreams left Martin in a sweat and the hand again reaching for the soft female flesh of his wife or girlfriend.

After just a few days, the perverted persistence of the hand began to drain Martin. Drain his girlfriend. Drain the wife.

'Stop this instant,' his wife said, pushing the hand away.

'Martin, that's *enough*!' screeched the girlfriend.

But the hand would not listen.

'That's it, Martin Swain! You're sleeping in the spare room,' the wife said, throwing him a travel rug and turning her back.

'Oh, come on, love, I'll take you out for a nice dinner. No handies under the table . . . I promise!'

So he picked a restaurant where he and his girlfriend never ate and told the hand in no uncertain terms to behave itself. Things were going well. He'd ushered his wife into the restaurant with the hand nestled in the small of her back. No slipping downwards for a quick grab of her rear. At dinner he used his original hand to elegantly refill his wife's wine glass while he made the hairy hand grip the leg of the table.

'That's fine, darling,' he said smiling, 'order crayfish if you like. It's not too expensive at all.'

But as the waitress came back to take their orders, the hand flew out from under the table and up the waitress's short black skirt, grabbing a handful of young dimpled flesh. Martin, teeth gritted, pulled the hand away after the third scream. He found himself looking across the table at his seething wife through a film of stinging red wine, which the waitress had thrown in his face.

At home his wife locked herself in the ensuite and sobbed for hours. The next morning she emerged puffy-eyed to see Martin outside greeting their neighbour, Mrs Pottinghouse, as he picked up the paper from the drive. With horror, the wife saw Martin's newly stitched hand fling itself inside Mrs Pottinghouse's flannelette dressing-gown.

Martin's eyes locked with Mrs Pottinghouse's as they both screamed, Martin tugging frantically on his arm with his original hand to make the hairy hand release her voluminous, squelchy breast. After failing to satisfactorily explain the situation to Mr Pottinghouse, Martin went back into his house with a fresh black eye, fat lip and a ripped Ralph Lauren shirt. He found his wife in the bedroom amidst a flurry of clothes, which she was shoving into a suitcase. She slammed the door behind her as she left and made certain she grated the gears of the Mercedes as she sped off down the road.

Two months after the operation, Martin Swain, who had been slated for the top executive position with his company, was told in no uncertain terms to leave. It had started out well enough in the office. The congratulations over his operation, the condolences over his wife, the fascination and sympathy of the office girls, the fun and games over a simple hand-shake. But soon the women in the office ran for cover when Martin and his new hand came near. Now he was accused of sexual harassment on seventeen different counts. Eleven of the charges came from the girls in the office – even one from dotty old Dot, the receptionist. Other complaints flooded in from women taxi drivers, shop assistants, bottle-shop staff and even from a stripper in one of the more upmarket bars.

'Surely that one wouldn't count?' raved Martin to his lawyer.

Pleas to his surgeons, who were still basking in the glory of such a successful operation, fell on deaf ears.

'But why can't you remove it and replace it with the hand of an artist or a great engineer? Anything! Just get rid of this one!' he yelled at his doctor.

Martin was sent to counselling. That was until the stern-jawed, elegant counsellor was made to shriek and run from her office with the hand and a horrified Martin following.

The final straw for Martin was when his girlfriend left

him. Or rather kicked him out of her duplex home. He had thought his girlfriend would always stand by him.

'Martin,' she said waving her hairbrush at him, 'in the early days I chose to ignore your troubles. I ignored the charges, put up with your sacking, and held you in my arms when your car and house were repossessed. But I cannot, *simply cannot*, ignore you grabbing the pizza girl. And what's more,' she screamed, 'I cannot put up with *this*!'

She flicked the remote control and to the TV screen sprang the neat newsreader telling viewers about Martin Swain's sexual harassment charges. The final straw for the girlfriend had been when the nightly news crew trampled her gladioli flower bed as they scrambled to get the best shot of Martin leaving her house for court. She took her protests to the TV station's head office. It was there she met the suit-clad newsreader with the dazzling smile and stunning hairdo.

No, she said with a gleeful smile, she didn't mind at all if they went for coffee to discuss the finer points of the story.

When Martin had called his surgeon at home in desperation he nearly gagged when he heard his wife's voice answer the phone. His new hand dropped the phone. As he sat sobbing outside the phone box with his head in his original hand, he hardly noticed the warm, wet sensation of a dog lifting its leg on him.

Now in the flat in the dark, with only the fuzzy light from the TV, Martin Swain, with a kitchen knife in his original hand, tries in vain, yet again, to sever the hand which was never his.

Evie's Garden Dreaming

Evie knew Barnaby was depressed by the way the old dog sighed. The rust-tinged kelpie spent his days at the window, gazing out beyond the potted herbs on Evie's small patio and up to the smog-filled sky. Today, misty rain clouds hung above the units and washed out the morning with their drabness. Barnaby sank his head between his greying front paws and gave another sad sigh. Evie glanced at him and sighed herself. It was ridiculous keeping a farm dog cooped up in the city.

With a cup of homegrown ginger tea, Evie settled into a snug armchair that had tufts of horsehair sprouting like whiskers from its sides. She recalled with a smile the way the farm cats used to scratch at the chair. It was one of a pair, taken from the rambling old farmhouse where she had lived on the outskirts of Melbourne.

'You won't fit both the chairs in your new unit, Mum,' her daughter Trish had said firmly, after the farm was sold. 'You can keep one and I'll have it reupholstered for you in a lovely chintz.'

Evie ran her cracked old fingertips over the chair's leather, which was as dry as dust. She smiled gently, and her husband smiled back at her from behind the glass of a photo frame. In the photo, Henry was perched on an old apple bin in the dapple of a summer orchard, his eyes crinkled in a joyful smile and his strong arms wrapped around a young, waggy-tailed Barnaby. Evie often talked to Henry.

'I wonder if someone's pruned the orchard trees yet, dear?' she said to Henry's image. Barnaby cocked an ear at the sound of her voice.

Evie's son-in-law, Neil, had set aside the city unit for Evie after Henry died. Trish had driven out to the farm especially to tell her, stepping from her BMW in a waft of Joy.

Evie was in the kitchen bottling raspberry jam the colour of blood, while Barnaby lay on a small cloud of sheepskin near the wood-fired stove. Trish settled herself at the table and watched Evie put the blackened kettle on the stove.

'Neil's got a special deal on one of the properties he's developed in Port Melbourne,' Trish said. 'It's a lovely sunny space right next to the beach. You'll love it, Mum. And the best thing is that because his business partners are overseas investors, they'll never object to you keeping an old dog. The other residents and the body corporate will turn a blind eye too, because Neil is . . . well, he's Neil.'

Yes, thought Evie, Neil was a powerful man. So high up the ladder it seemed he never actually worked at anything, except talking into his tiny, bullet-like cell phone. In the summer, he buzzed around Port Phillip Bay on his jet ski, wearing his reflector sunglasses and looking like a Monaco royal. But it was winter now and Neil and Trish had taken the four-wheel drive to Mount Hotham for the snow. Instead of surfing the white crests of salty waves, Neil was surfing white snowdrifts down the mountain. What he didn't see from behind his sunglasses was that long after the snow had melted and tumbled down to the river far below, the mountainside was left brown, its compacted soil lifeless and dull. It was how the murky bottom of Port Phillip Bay must look too, Evie mused; a watery desert of crown-of-thorns starfish and sewage, where once a seaweed-green forest had thrived. But Neil would never think like that.

Evie glanced at the bay from her front window. On most days, she preferred to draw her curtains to shut out the traffic and her view of the grubby grey sand that needed to be combed of its rubbish every day. When Evie and Barnaby did venture out, they slipped through the jagged hole in a high mesh fence beside the unit complex to reach the vacant block next door. The block was a no-man's land, a large barren square choked with weeds and rubble. It was land on hold until Neil gathered more money from overseas so he could stack concrete up high with his mighty machines. Part of a tumbledown fibro house was all that stood after the dozers retreated. A half-house looking like a half-eaten cake.

But, Evie thought, at least the block could conjure the memory of a summer paddock for Barnaby, with golden grassy wisps brushing against his flanks. Picking up her tea, Evie sighed again at the same time as her dog.

At the rear of the units was a large expanse of perfect lawn bordered by neat garden beds. The upper-storey windows overlooked the garden like unseeing eyes. Each unit had a tiny terrace fenced off with high vertical bars. Some residents grew jasmine over the bars, others roses, while still others arranged giant pots with nothing in them. It was all very tidy. No one seemed to be home much, Evie observed, and it was always so quiet except when the young maintenance man came and broke the silence with his whipper snipper, electric hedge trimmers, rattling wheelie bins and his leaf blower.

'The security system here is fantastic,' Trish had said the day she brought Evie to the unit. 'And the complex has both an indoor and an outdoor pool. Plus a sauna and gym.'

Trish had giggled at the gym part. Evie knew the thought of an eighty-something-year-old lady working out on a step machine was funny for Trish. Evie laughed along with her daughter.

Trish hadn't spent much time on the farm after she left

home for university, so Trish didn't know that beneath her mother's loose-fitting shirt and trousers was a body that defied Evie's true age. She was greyhound-slim and her strong bones were supported by lean muscles. Country life had shaped her like no gym could. Evie's snow-white hair sat like a sunny-day cloud above her radiant blue eyes. Her sun-speckled skin was as patterned and imperfect as a landscape. Etched on her face was her love of hard work and laughter.

In her life with Henry, there had been daily milkings, hoeing weeds in the vegetable plots and helping Henry lug crates full of apples to sell at the local market, along with fresh eggs, pats of creamy butter and jars of golden honey. Then there'd be Saturday nightcaps of homemade wine, she and Henry both a bit tiddly, and dancing together to old-time music.

They'd bought the red kelpie pup they named Barnaby not long after Trish left the farm. When Henry and Evie dipped their hands into the cool red soil to grub out potatoes, Barnaby would wait, paws splayed and tail wagging at the sky. Then Henry would toss a potato his way. Catching it in his mouth, Barnaby would lie beneath the giant eucalypt, roll the spud between his paws and fling it high in the air in his own joyous game of fetch.

Evie and Barnaby were dozing when the rev of a leaf blower ripped through the unit and startled them awake. Then, as it was right on midday, Evie heard the automatic watering system switch on. It came on every day, rain, hail or shine.

She watched the sprinklers raise their shiny black plastic heads from the lawns like alien worms as they spat water onto already sodden grass. Barnaby had his ears flattened to block out the droning invasion of the leaf blower. Poor Barnaby, Evie thought, this wouldn't do.

As the maintenance man came nearer, leaves blasted against the window and Evie couldn't help but wish she was in that peaceful place where she imagined Henry to be. A place of heaven: green clover, sunshine and the cooling shade of giant leafy trees. Outside her window, the manmade wind lifted curled old leaves in gusting eddies.

'Strong enough to blow feathers off a chook,' said Evie. Then a vision came to her mind and she sat bolt upright in her chair. She remembered the way Barnaby would manoeuvre the chooks into a group with the concentration of a chess player, and herd them into the henhouse on dusk. He always barked at the last feathery tuft of tail as it disappeared as if to say, 'Checkmate!'

Evie smiled, as ideas began to flow as fast as the water that had raced along their farm's creek bed after days of spring rain. It was as if the weight of her new city world had lifted from her shoulders and she was flying free. She picked up her husband's photo and embraced it.

'Henry, darling,' she said, 'that leaf-blowing man has given me the most wonderful idea. And it all begins with chooks, Henry. Chooks!' She stood and waved hello to the maintenance man. He saw her, removed his yellow earmuffs for a moment, and smiled uncertainly before resuming his blowing.

The next day when the bell rang, Barnaby was at the door first, his tail wagging. He could smell them. Chooks! A sturdy man stood at the door with a large box.

'Where you want chicken?' he asked with an accent as thick as molasses. It must be the same foreign gentleman Evie had talked to yesterday.

She showed him around the side of her unit, where she'd deftly wired off an enclosure and set up some plastic garbage bins as makeshift nesting boxes. No one would notice a couple of chooks, she thought, not tucked away beside the building like this.

Things worked like clockwork here. The man from unit twelve got his morning paper at 6.10 a.m. The woman from unit two went for her morning jog at 6.30. The corner unit man walked on the beach with the lady from unit seven at 6.45. And then everyone left for work, their cars shooting out from the underground car park to be swallowed up by a slow, gleaming snake of traffic.

It was just the maintenance man who seemed to be about most of the day. He'd arrive, a little after nine, in a haze of blue smoke from his old Mazda. He was young and lean and a little lazy, Evie suspected, and had long hair like she'd seen on Corriedale rams. He always took two hours off at lunch and never spoke to her, even when she said hello. Evie decided that the chooks could roam about the garden during his long lunch break, and Barnaby would herd them back in each day.

The poultry deliveryman set the box down.

'Here?' he said looking at the makeshift chicken run as if Evie were mad.

'Yes, here,' nodded Evie enthusiastically.

'Hokay.' He frowned, shrugged his broad shoulders and set the box down. 'I get other box.' He strode out to his van.

How kind of them to put a hen each in such big boxes, thought Evie. As the man set down the second box and handed Evie the bill she nearly choked. Chooks had never cost that much in the country, but still, everything seemed dearer here, and she supposed that's what people in the city did . . . they shopped. If it made Barnaby happy, she didn't care. She wrote out the cheque, her glasses slipping down the bridge of her fine nose. Evie waited until the man had left before opening the boxes.

'Good Lord!' she gasped. There, squashed in the box, were a dozen hens. She opened the second box, which was also packed full. Two dozen hens!

'But there's been a misunderstanding, Henry. I said a couple of chooks . . . not a couple of dozen!' She imagined Henry up in heaven on a cloud laughing. He always saw the funny side.

She was about to call the poultry place when she noticed how miserable the chickens looked. Their feathers, normally the delicious colour of Anzac biscuits, were dull. They had red-raw patches of bare skin on their necks. Even though the lids of the boxes were wide open, the hens were too terrified to venture out into the misty rain. Evie couldn't send them back. Not now. The poor girls. And there was Barnaby lying on his belly, ears pricked, tail wagging at the very tip, every cell in his body bursting for his work to begin. The brightest he'd been in months.

Evie looked through the bars of her garden to the maintenance man in the courtyard. He'd stopped leaf-blowing and was now pruning the spindly leaves of an exotic orange flower that looked like the beak of a tropical bird.

'Excuse me, young man,' Evie called as she unlatched the gate and walked towards him. 'I have a problem and I thought you might like to help.'

Later, with Oliver seated at her small outdoor table, his pruning shears laid down beside him, Evie offered another homemade scone the colour of soft sunshine.

'It would just be until their feathers grow back and they've learnt to scratch the soil,' she said. 'Then I can find good homes for them.'

Oliver pushed up the sleeves of his blue work shirt and frowned. 'A chicken run, here? It could cost me my job,' he said gruffly.

'Surely that wouldn't be too bad a thing?' Evie said gently. 'A fit young man like you could get work anywhere.'

'I'm trying to save money though,' Oliver said, sinking his white teeth into a scone.

'May I ask what for?' Evie drizzled golden honey into Oliver's tea. It was the last of the honey Henry had collected from the beehives in the orchard before he died.

'I'm going on an eco-activists tour next year,' Oliver said keenly.

'Oh? What's that, dear?'

'You know, organised environmental protests. We're starting down in Tasmania for logging protests, then there's a trip to the Victorian mountains to protest about cattle up there, then there's a sit-in against wind farms near the Prom, then another out west to protest about water taken from the river systems for irrigation . . . and then back home to Melbourne. Environment's what I'm passionate about, but for the time being I'm working here. Just for the money. You know.'

'Yes, I think I do know,' Evie said. She set down her cup and glanced out at the regimented garden beyond the bars of her patio before turning to Oliver. 'My dear, do you think we could put your plans aside – just for now – and make a start in our own garden? For the moment we've got twenty-four sad chooks and there's all that space out there that they can't use.'

Oliver sighed.

'But I've never been on a farm. I don't know anything about chickens.'

'Don't worry, Barnaby and I will teach you. And while we get our girls settled, I'll fill you in on a few more of my ideas . . . because I have a grander plan to hatch,' Evie said with a twinkle in her eye. 'If you'll pardon the pun.'

———————◆———————

Oliver pressed a button on Evie's brand-new printer and began printing out the *Notice to Residents* Evie had composed. Trish had bought Evie the computer but until now it had lain dormant in the corner of the room, like a sleeping beast. Oliver handed Evie the freshly printed page.

'The body corporate won't like this at all when they find out,' he said.

'They won't see it coming till it's already done,' Evie said. 'That's the beauty of a grassroots revolution.'

She read over the letter, which informed residents of the forthcoming 'landscape garden changes', beginning with a 'central garden feature' of a 'stylish and modern chicken coop'. The letter went on to offer residents a unique share in the community chicken rehabilitation project. All they had to do was contribute household food scraps to the specially labelled bin in the car park. Oliver would collect the bin daily and feed the chooks. In return, residents could collect free-range eggs at no charge from Evie in unit ten.

———————◆———————

And so it began. Neighbours came and gingerly knocked on Evie's door. She welcomed them with the smell of fresh-baked bread and a smile as lively and intriguing as life itself. And as the wintry days unfolded into spring, things began to change.

The chickens gained their feathers and lost their fear. They began to scratch about while Oliver and Evie worked side by side in the garden. As Oliver's hands sunk into the rich dark soil he no longer talked about protests in places he'd never lived. He began to see the land and nature for the first time, right here at his fingertips in the centre of the city. Old Barnaby was happier too as he dozed beneath a white-trunked sapling, keeping one foggy eye on the chooks. Then, at dusk, he'd wait for Evie to ask him to herd the chooks away to roost.

The residents came to watch and wonder at Barnaby's expert moves, so gentle yet so firm. The man from unit twelve became Vern and the woman from unit two became Rita. Even Dennis, from unit five, who didn't eat eggs, still brought his scraps down from level two in an old blue ice-cream bucket. As the residents delivered their scraps, collected their eggs, made up names for the chickens and stroked their glossy feathers, they began to laugh and trust and talk to each other.

By the time the buds of spring had stretched into the leafy green of summer, Evie and Oliver had dug up most of the soil and even the lawns. They planted herbs, lettuces and other vegetables in designs as intricate as lace. Peas and beans entwined themselves up and over the bars of people's patios, rich green threads woven by sunlight. Deep-crimson leaves of beetroot flanked pathways alongside rows of upright glossy silverbeet. The green-gold of butter beans led residents into the garden's heart, where the outdoor swimming pool now teemed with trout. Tendrils of passionfruit vines clutched upwards for a better view of Evie's garden that now rambled and sang with vitality and life-giving food.

In the evenings, the residents gathered on the pool's edge and fished together. Men sat in deck chairs, landing fish as silver as new coins. The women chatted while snapping the shells of peas and spooling out their sweet green orbs. The smell of melting butter and fresh fish on the barbecue hotplate drifted up from the courtyard.

The residents strolled amidst the fledgling orchard and inspected where the grey water seeped from a snake of black pipe. And the residents felt good that they now fed the garden with water from their own sinks and showers.

One such summer's evening, Evie and the other residents asked Oliver to help them cut the fence between them and the vacant block. After that, the garden seemed to spill out into the wasteland, so that a pretty patchwork of corn and sunflowers and carrots were sown in with other vegetables. On the block the residents, hoed, carted, dug and sweated, while the equipment in the gym lay silent.

There was a buzz about the place the day Rita from unit two announced she had a cousin with a cow or two.

'Since the Royal Show closed down, he can't show them any more and he'd like us to have them,' Rita said as she plucked parsnips from the soil.

When the cows arrived, the residents were in awe of their quiet, matronly beauty. Vera was a Jersey with eyes like melted chocolate, and Amelia was a Friesian with ears as black as midnight and a belly as white as a dove, both with equally pretty calves at foot.

They tethered them next door on the vacant block. That day, Evie swept the rubble and dust out of the ramshackle half-house. Oliver gathered up the rubbish of cans, needles and old wine casks. And together they built a milking bale and filled it with sweet-smelling straw.

Twice a day, the cows wandered in, chewed happily on hay and listened to the sound of their milk zinging into buckets as Evie and Oliver milked them. Children began to sneak into the garden to stroke the white star on Amelia's face and to see their own faces mirrored within Vera's deep brown eyes. Peter from unit six would cart the fresh milk to the courtyard and the residents rolled up their sleeves to make cheese and butter and skim off the cream. Laughter rose up from Evie's garden even on days when rain fell. On wet days, the people no longer scuttled for their units. Instead, they stood out in it as Evie did, because they now understood that the rain was life-giving. As was the food their garden now grew.

It was late when Evie said good night to everyone. They had all been busy, preparing the plots for more plantings. Evie poured herself a port and sank into her old leather chair. Barnaby settled his head on her lap and she rested her hand on his warm head. Then, Evie raised her glass to Henry's photo.

'Here's to you, my darling farmer, for your love. And here's cheers to Mother Nature, a very wise lady.' Evie drank happily from the glass and, with a smile on her lips, fell into a blissful sleep.

———◦•◦———

Trish knocked and knocked on the unit door. No answer came from within. When she slid the spare key in the lock and pushed open the door she almost gagged. The staleness of the flat and the way Barnaby slunk past her legs and out onto the street told her everything she needed to know.

'Mum?' she called out, knowing for certain Evie wouldn't answer.

Trish couldn't bring herself to look at her mother, dead in the chair, still clutching a photograph of her husband. Instead she called the ambulance right away from her mobile as she stood in the doorway.

Later, still hovering near the front door, Trish spoke to the blue-uniformed men who'd come in the ambulance. She was dabbing her eyes with a crisp white handkerchief, pulled from within the belly of a snakeskin handbag.

'I haven't been in for a while,' she said. 'Very busy, you know. My husband and I are away a lot . . . on business. But we made sure she had everything she needed.' She shook her head. 'It's a wonder the neighbours didn't notice anything. Surely they could've called someone when they hadn't seen her about for a few days?'

The ambos nodded at her and one muttered, 'You'd be surprised how often elderly people aren't missed for days on end.'

Trish looked out onto the street where cars raced past in a rush.

'I've no idea where that damn dog went. If you see him let me know.'

'Sure,' said the ambulance driver, unlocking the brake on the stainless-steel trolley. 'Now if you don't mind, we'll take her out the back way, through the garden. We couldn't get parking out the front.'

As Trish gingerly entered the apartment, she stooped to pick up the phone book that lay open beside the chair. She frowned, wondering why on earth her mother would have circled *Poultry* in the Yellow Pages.

When they wheeled Evie's body through the garden and along the pathway, the man doing laps in the pool didn't stop. The bronzed woman lying on a sun lounge talked into her mobile phone and didn't look up. Then, as they opened the gate from the garden, a leaf blower roared into action. It was right on midday when the men shut the doors of the ambulance. The automatic sprinklers popped up and began to water the lawn. And out on the street, no one seemed to care that an old red kelpie was dodging traffic and loping, terrified, into the heart of the city.

Days later, Barnaby arrived. He arrived with the pads of his paws bleeding and bruised and with concrete-worn claws. His nerves were jangled by noise and his stomach rumbled from hunger. The old dog stood at the entrance to Evie and Henry's farm, his tongue hanging out, his ribs showing beneath his dull coat. He slumped down where the large gum tree used to be.

In its place above him towered a sign. *Red Gums Estate – The Best of Country Living. Contact Neil or Trish for investment details.*

Barnaby sighed and sniffed the petrol-filled air. Beyond the sign, stretching as far as his old eyes could see, were rows of orange-tiled roofs, one after the other, and on and on.

Hours later, a ute pulled out of the stream of traffic and rolled to a stop. Barnaby lifted his head from the concrete where he lay. A young man stepped out and crouched down. Barnaby could smell it, the smell of soil and fresh air and the best thing of all . . . chooks! He wagged his tail.

'What's an old bloke like you doing in a place like this?' the man said. 'You lost?'

Barnaby heaved himself to his feet and looked at the young man.

'Your guardian angel must be lookin' after you today, fella,' the man said. 'C'mon, we'll get some soil under your paws. I'll take you somewhere you belong.' He scooped up the dog and laid him gently on the seat of his ute. And then they drove away, away from the place where Evie and Henry's farm used to be.

Also by Rachael Treasure

Jillaroo

After a terrible argument with her father over their family property, 'Waters Meeting', Rebecca Saunders throws her swag in the ute and heads north with her three dogs. A job as a jillaroo takes her into the rowdy world of B&S balls, Bundy rum and boys. When she at last settles down to a bit of study at agricultural college, her life is turned upside down by the very handsome but very drunken party animal Charlie Lewis . . .

Will she choose a life of wheat farming on vast open plains with Charlie? Or will she return to the mountains, to fight for the land and the river that runs through her soul?

It's only when tragedy shatters her world that Rebecca finds a strength and courage she never knew she had, in this action-packed novel of adventure, dreams and determination.

'By the end of this book, you yearn for a ute, a pair of boots and the wide open spaces.'

AUSTRALIAN WOMEN'S WEEKLY

The Stockmen

Rosie Highgrove-Jones grows up hating her double-barrelled name. She dreams of riding out over the wide plains of the family property, working on the land. Instead she's stuck writing the social pages of the local paper.

Then a terrible tragedy sparks a series of shocking revelations for Rosie and her family. As she tries to put her life back together, Rosie throws herself into researching the haunting true story of a nineteenth-century Irish stockman who came to Australia and risked his all for a tiny pup and a wild dream. Is it just coincidence when Rosie meets a sexy Irish stockman of her own? And will Jim help her realise her deepest ambitions – or will he break her heart?

The Stockmen moves effortlessly between the present and the past to reveal a simple yet hard-won truth – that both love and the land are timeless . . .

The Rouseabout

Kate Webster is a loveable larrikin who likes to play hard now and worry about the consequences later. She can't help mucking up the opportunities life gives her. Rocked by the death of her mother, she takes on a dare at one of Australia's wildest rural social events – a Bachelors & Spinsters ball – to 'scalp' gorgeous farm boy Nick McDonnell. It's a dare that changes everything. For just as Kate is ready to start her new life, away from her grieving father and the pressures of the family farm, she discovers she is pregnant. Now, several years later, with toddler Nell by her side, it's time for Kate to come home to face the music – and the father of her child . . .

Set on the beautiful island of Tasmania, where Rachael Treasure once kicked up her own heels at B&S balls, *The Rouseabout* is an unforgettable story about discovering the things that truly matter, and finding love that lasts.

'A heartwarming look at women on the land.'
WHO WEEKLY

'Kate is a true Aussie heroine.'
NEWCASTLE HERALD

The Cattleman's Daughter

Born on the rugged Dargo High Plains and raised by her cattleman father, Emily Flanaghan has lost her way in life.

Locked in an unhappy marriage in the suburbs, Emily misses the high country with a fierce ache. To make matters worse, her heritage is under threat. A government bill to evict the mountain cattlemen is about to be passed, and the Flanaghans could be banned from the mountains their family has looked after for generations.

When a terrible accident brings Emily to the brink of death, she realises she must return to the high country to seek a way forward in life, healing herself, her daughters and her land. Along the way, she finds herself falling in love with a man who works for the government – the traditional opposition of the cattlemen – new Parks ranger, Luke Bradshaw. But just as she sees that the land and Luke are the keys to regaining her life, Emily faces losing them both in the greatest challenge of all . . .

Set in the beautiful snowgum country of the Victorian Alps, *The Cattleman's Daughter* is a haunting and unforgettable tale of love, self-discovery and forgiveness from one of Australia's best-loved authors.